SURROUNDED
BY THE CROSS FIRE

---•---

PETER REESE DOYLE

PUBLISHING

Colorado Springs, Colorado

SURROUNDED BY THE CROSS FIRE

International copyright secured.

Library of Congress Cataloging-in-Publication Data
Doyle, Peter Reese, 1930-

    Surrounded By the Cross Fire / Peter Reese Doyle.

    p. cm—(Daring Family adventures ; 4)

    Summary: The Darings experience thrills and chills when they interrupt a drug runner's operation in France.

    ISBN 1-56179-258-6

    [1. Adventure and adventurers—Fiction. 2.France—Fiction.

3. Christian life—Fiction] I. Title. II. Series: Doyle, Peter

Reese, 1930-   Daring Family adventures : bk.. 4.

PZ7.D777Sur 1994

[Fic]—dc20

Published by Focus on the Family Publishing, Colorado Springs, Colorado 80995.

Distributed by Word Books, Dallas, Texas.

Editor: Etta Wilson
Designer: James A. Lebbad
Cover Illustration: Ken Spengler

Printed in the United States of America
94 95 96 97 98 99 / 10 9 8 7 6 5 4 3 2 1

For

Dee Dee

Who raised us, taught us to pray,
and loves and inspires us still.

CONTENTS

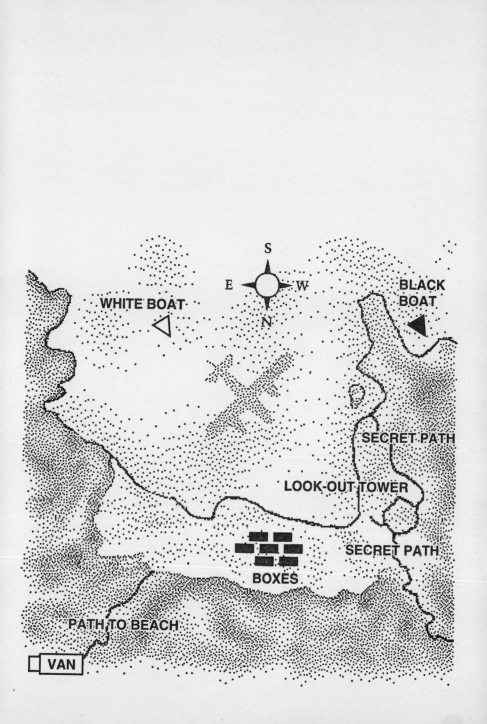

CHAPTER 1

DOWN AT SEA!

The second engine sputtered, coughed—and died! The first had already gone.

Instantly the near-silence in the plane's cabin was terrifying. All that could be heard was the whining of the wind outside. The moonless night seemed to close in on them with deadly threat.

"How far to the shore?" the pilot snapped, his hand flying to the trim controls, seeking to fine-tune the craft for its glide to the sea. He had to coax every possible yard of flight out of the plane before it hit the water.

"Too far," the copilot said bleakly, flipping on a small cockpit light and frantically scanning the map taped to his knee. "Too far," he repeated, his voice strained. "We'll never make it."

They could almost smell the fear mingled with the grease, electrical wiring, and leather in the cabin of the twin-engine private plane.

The darkened aircraft had been skimming the Mediterranean at an altitude of three hundred feet, seeking to avoid the radar of ships and the coastal stations of southern France. When the right-hand engine conked out, however, the pilot had climbed for altitude, risking detection, knowing he had to have as much coasting distance as possible if his remaining engine quit.

That had been ten minutes ago. Now the plane, with no power, sliced through the air in as narrow a glide as the pilot could manage. He was desperately seeking to reach the coast and the small airstrip where the vans waited to receive the smuggled drugs on board the plane.

"We'll never make it," the copilot repeated, fear giving a whine to his voice. He had always hated these night flights.

"Shut up! I'm not giving up," the pilot snapped back.

The beach was not far away, actually, but could they reach it? Before taking off with their load of drugs from the secluded North African field, they'd plotted the course with care. They had noted the small beach on the coast of southern France toward which they were headed. They'd seen that the beach was bordered by high rock outcroppings—like guard towers—on either end. There were no real roads to the area, just a rough narrow path barely passable for cars or trucks. Better yet, there were no towns nearby.

The men had planned to skim the water above the secluded guarded beach, swerve 20 degrees east, follow this course for 60 kilometers, then land, without circling, in a level field where the vans were waiting. The fuel truck would fill up their tanks while the 40 gray boxes in the plane's baggage compartment were being loaded into the waiting vans.

Then the aircraft would take off and return to Africa the way it had come, flying under the radar until safely past the North African shore. That would make another successful trip; another load of the priceless drugs brought illegally into Europe; another tremendous sum of money earned. This was the last trip for this crew. Only fools pushed their luck!

But things hadn't worked out as they'd planned. And now, without power, they were desperately seeking to glide as far as they could toward the coast of France.

With infinite care and great skill the pilot directed the plane on its course, holding it up as long as he could, skimming as far as its weight and aerodynamic capacities allowed, hoping to get as close as possible to that hidden beach. He was thankful that this was a propeller plane and not a jet. Jets had all the gliding capacities of a rock!

"If we can glide far enough," he said, "we can land in the water just off the beach, swim to shore, and come back for the cargo later. The water's not too deep for diving. No one should spot the plane under the water in this deserted spot. We can still get that cargo and still be rich!"

The copilot didn't reply. Fighting to control his fear, he'd unbuckled his belt, gone back into the pitch-dark cabin, and readied the life belts and raft. He returned to the seat and with shaking hands rebuckled his belt.

"Maybe we'll make it," he said. The darkness in the cabin was terrible. His shirt and trousers were soaked with sweat from his fear, but he didn't panic. He couldn't panic!

"We'll make it," the pilot said firmly.

Suddenly before their anxious eyes there appeared through the darkness ahead the gleam of sandy beach between towering piles of rock on either side. The water below was dark. There was no way the pilot could tell what the surface of the sea was like: it could be smooth as glass or wild and choppy. They wouldn't know until they hit.

They *had* to make a smooth landing! If they didn't, they'd strike a wave, somersault, and the plane would fall to pieces. Then they would never get out alive.

"Here goes," the pilot said, pulling back the wheel, lifting the nose of the plane slightly, setting the gliding craft down in the pitch-black darkness as the tall rock cliffs ahead rushed toward them with terrifying speed.

CHAPTER 2

FIRST—
MARSEILLE

The taxi pulled to the curb. Mark paid the driver; then he jumped out and followed Penny and David up the steps to the hotel entrance. The three teenagers moved quickly inside and crossed the lobby to the open elevator. David punched the button for the third floor.

"I hope they're ready!" Penny said anxiously, as the elevator began to ascend.

"Don't worry," her brother, Mark, replied. "They'll be ready. Did you ever know Mom and Dad to be late?"

A powerfully built young man of seventeen, Mark Daring stood five feet eleven in his socks. Blond with a broad, friendly face, he was a year older than his sister Penny. His muscled frame filled his dark slacks and light shirt.

Penny Daring, her face framed by light brown hair that fell to her shoulders, was five feet seven and slender in her green jumper and white blouse. She had a dimple when she smiled—which was often—and David thought she was the most beautiful girl alive. He didn't dare tell her this, of course!

David Curtis had flown from the States to visit Mark and Penny in Africa. Then their parents had brought him along with them to Paris where Mr. Daring had business. Taller than Mark by two inches, David was lean and also powerfully muscled.

After the teenagers' desperate escape from a gang in the catacombs below the great French capital, Mrs. Daring had insisted that they go to Carcassone for some rest and a *safe* vacation. They planned to leave Paris by the famous fast train within the hour, traveling first to the great Mediterranean seaport of Marseille, and then to the historic city of Carcassone, several days later.

The three chatted happily as the elevator ascended, eager to begin the trip to the south of France. They'd packed that morning and then visited their favorite outdoor restaurant for an hour while Mr. and Mrs. Daring got ready. Now they'd come back to the hotel to go with the Darings to the train station.

None of the teenagers had seen the taxi that had followed their own from the outdoor restaurant where they'd had a last chocolate éclair before leaving Paris. This taxi had screeched to a stop just as the three Americans walked into the hotel. Two men jumped out, one rushing toward the hotel entrance while the other shoved a fistful of franc notes at the driver and told him to wait.

The first man walked quickly into the hotel lobby,

just in time to see the elevator door close behind Mark, Penny, and David. Realizing he couldn't catch up, he changed course, slowed his pace, and sauntered toward the desk as if he had all the time in the world.

Behind the desk, a middle-aged woman in a drab black dress was answering the phone when the tall, sharply dressed man walked up. For several minutes she ignored him while he stared at her grey hair pulled back into a bun. Inwardly the tall man fumed; outwardly he was the picture of patience and charm, standing elegantly in his expensive dark suit.

Finally she put the receiver down, shuffled the papers before her, and, without looking up, asked in a bored voice, "Oui, monsieur?"

His long face broke into a friendly smile, which was lost on the woman.

Patiently the man explained his problem. He and his friend had been sitting at an outdoor cafe where one of three American teenagers left a very expensive fountain pen at the adjoining table. He wished to return this valuable writing instrument, and had taken a taxi and followed them here. But the young people had just gotten into the elevator as he'd entered the lobby, and he couldn't catch them in time. Unfortunately, he didn't even know their names. Could she help him locate them so he could give them their expensive pen?

Wearily the woman told Sergei that the teenagers were the children of an American family named Daring. She gave him the room number so he could call them from the lobby floor. "They're leaving for Marseille this morning," she added.

"Oh?" he replied, one eyebrow rising. "Merci beaucoup."

He walked rapidly to a bank of phones on the far wall, his mind racing. How could he retrieve that letter from the girl's camera case if the family was going to Marseille in an hour? They *had* to retrieve that letter!

His partner, meanwhile, had sauntered into the lobby and sat down on a sofa, where he pretended to read a paper. Actually he was watching the elevator as well as the hotel entrance.

Before dialing, Sergei looked back. The desk clerk was now on the telephone herself, and wouldn't be able to hear his conversation. Ignoring the room number she'd given him, he proceeded to dial an outside number instead. How could he explain his failure to get that letter? He began to sweat. The KGB did not appreciate agents who did not accomplish their mission!

A mile away, in another part of Paris, Schmidt, a heavyset man, let the phone ring: once, twice, three times. Then it stopped. Schmidt waited, setting down his coffee.

An ashtray filled with cigarette butts flanked the phone he'd been staring at for the past half hour. The crude wooden table at which he sat was covered with a dirty green cloth stained with coffee and food. The air in the small room was stifling and stale as if the window and door hadn't been opened for months. Dark hangings covered the tall window, two lamps stood beside the large desk, and the heavy chair on which he sat was matched by an ugly brown sofa across the room. The phone rang again: once, twice, three times. His hand reached for it and hung poised in the air. When the phone rang again, Schmidt picked it up. "Oui?"

Schmidt's voice was deep, rasping. Years of smoking had taken their toll on his vocal cords. His doctor had warned him about this, but he'd refused to listen. Although he spoke in French, it was clearly not his native language.

"Sergei here," the tall man said from the lobby of the hotel. His French, on the contrary, was fluent, colloquial, polished. But his voice shook as he carefully chose the words to report his failure.

"Did you get that list?" Schmidt demanded instantly, eagerness giving a strange edge to his rasping voice.

"Not yet—" Sergei began. Then he winced and held the phone away from his ear as the angry curses burned the wire between them. Finally, he was allowed to explain.

Sergei told how the woman he'd followed had taken an awful chance, placing the letter with a list of agents in an open pocket of a stranger's camera case at a table adjoining hers. She was determined not to give Sergei that letter until the KGB had released her son. But the owner of the camera had left the restaurant before the woman had noticed, and Sergei had been fortunate to see the disappearing camera case just as the girl carrying it had entered a taxi. By the most strenuous efforts he and his fellow agent had managed to follow the three Americans to their hotel. And by his cleverness, he'd just learned their name and room number.

But he'd also learned that the Americans were about to leave for Marseille on the fast train! Now Sergei needed help to retrieve that letter. "We can follow them on the train and take another compartment. But we need someone in Marseille to watch for them in case we miss them in the station."

With great disgust, but greater urgency, Schmidt mapped out his plan. "Follow them! Steal that camera case if you can. I'll have agents meet you in Marseille. They'll steal it in the station if you haven't been able to do so. The station in Marseille is a perfect place for us to retrieve that case. People get robbed there every day! But if that fails, look for an opportunity to grab the case from the girl as the family tours the city. Or steal it from her room while they eat their meals. But, however you do it, that letter *must* be recovered!"

Schmidt decided that he'd better explain. "You know what would happen to us if the police got that list of names! They will arrest all of us for questioning!" His raspy voice could not conceal his anger.

Sergei winced at the consequences to them if they failed. Twenty people in their espionage network would be rounded up at once. Twenty people who had not been revealed by the KGB leaders to the new civilian rulers of Russia. Twenty KGB spies in the heart of Paris the most influential city in the world! That espionage ring *must not be exposed*! The time would come when the present fumbling democratic leaders would be removed from what had once been the Soviet Union. They'd be replaced by those who knew how to rule an empire. Until then, the KGB had to keep their intelligence units operating—and intact. And that meant undetected. Sergei knew how important this was!

"Here they come!" Sergei said suddenly. "I'll call when I can!" He jammed the phone into the receiver, leaned casually against the wall, and watched Mr. and Mrs. Daring, Mark, Penny, and David cross the lobby and leave the hotel. His comrade, Uri, put down his paper, rose leisurely from the sofa, and looked inquiringly at Sergei.

Sergei nodded and strolled to the door. From here he saw that the Americans were just getting into a taxi. Sergei waited until the taxi pulled away from the curb and moved into traffic. Then he dropped his casual pose and raced down the steps with Uri close behind him. Flinging open the door of the waiting, cab they tumbled in hurriedly.

"Follow that taxi ahead of you!" Sergei snapped.

As the two taxis headed for the train station, none of the Americans noticed the vehicle following them through the city's hectic traffic.

CHAPTER 3

THIEF!

The station at Marseille was mobbed with passengers rushing to and from the trains. "Don't get run over!" Jim Daring warned his family as they prepared to step out of the train. Mr. and Mrs. Daring went first, followed by Penny and the boys. They joined the crowds of people who'd left from the fast train and were now heading for the baggage section in the station.

"Keep your hands on your purses, girls!" Mr. Daring reminded his wife and Penny—not for the first time!

The great seaport of Marseille was notorious for its thieves and pickpockets. Mr. Daring and the boys wore special wallets attached to their belts and tucked inside their clothes. Mrs. Daring and Penny held their purses, and Penny kept a hand on her red canvas camera case hung over her shoulder by its strap. David and Mark walked behind the others, bringing up the rear so that the ladies were protected in the midst of the swirling crowds.

Mr. Daring led them swiftly toward the baggage section of the terminal.

The two men who'd followed them from Paris were ten yards behind, but the Americans didn't know it. Sergei and Uri had traveled in another part of the train, and the Darings hadn't noticed that they were being followed. They had no reason to suspect that they would be.

Sergei's mind was racing. Would his boss have a team ready to meet the Americans at the station? It would be so simple if they could steal that camera case in the crowds near the trains before their quarry boarded a taxi to their hotel! But he didn't know the men in the Marseille team, and didn't expect to recognize anyone. If another agent had come to help him and Uri steal that camera case, he would have to identify himself to Sergei.

"Which woman has the case we want?" a stranger asked quietly, as he bumped roughly into Sergei. A lean figure in nondescript brown shirt and trousers with black beret, the man looked straight ahead and seemed to have forgotten Sergei. His long sallow face was expressionless, his eyes dark.

"The younger one, with the red case," Sergei replied quietly, vastly relieved that Schmidt had sent help! The man pulled quickly ahead of him, drawing closer to the Americans.

Now the Darings had come to an open place in the midst of the mobs of people swirling in groups and streams. Languages of all kinds filled the air with harsh sounds. Mark, behind Penny, had just been distracted by a pantomimist amusing the crowd for pay, but David was watching Penny and he saw it happen.

The man in brown swooped toward Penny, sharp knife flashing as he pulled the strap of her camera case toward him and sliced through it, yanking the case away in his other hand. Whirling to flee, he encountered David's instinctive karate kick in his stomach! Gasping, the thief collapsed, the knife falling from his hand, the camera case tumbling beside it.

"Mark!" David yelled, as he scooped up Penny's camera case and backed away from the man on the ground, in a fighting stance, looking to each side for other attackers. Mark whirled and stepped to David's side. Mr. Daring moved to join them while his wife and daughter came close behind. The family had discussed situations like this before and knew what to do. People scattered, flowing around the writhing man on the ground, hurrying to escape the scene of trouble and leave the station.

Sergei and Uri, still several yards behind, realized at once that the attempt had failed and they couldn't get involved. But Sergei's long stare caught David's eye. Instantly David realized that this man was somehow involved. The Russian looked away—but not before he'd aroused David's suspicions.

Sergei and Uri headed away quickly. Another man rushed to help the would-be thief to his feet, somehow recovering the knife from the ground and concealing it in his clothes. The crowds moved on and the Darings realized that this was too common an event to merit the attention of a policeman—if they could find one in the crowds!

As the thief and his helper disappeared, David spoke quickly. "That man's involved, Mark!" David said, pointing to Sergei as he and Uri disappeared in the mass of people.

"I'll remember him," Mark said grimly.

"Let's go," Mr. Daring said, leading his family toward the baggage claim area. They were all very alert now.

"Jim!" his wife exclaimed in shock. "How could danger

follow us here? Isn't there any place where these children will be safe?"

"It was just a common thief, I guess," her husband replied. "Remember, Henri Mevel warned us about thieves in this station." He turned to David. "That was quick work," he said, smiling with admiration at their young friend whose instant response had saved Penny's camera.

"It sure was!" Penny agreed, her eyes shining her thanks at David. "I suddenly felt the strap pulling away from me and I didn't know what had happened."

Later that evening, dining in a splendid restaurant, the family had almost forgotten the incident. The tour they'd taken before the late dinner had put it out of their minds; so had the fabulous French food. Now they were eating dessert.

"Penny, this chocolate pie is no better than what you bake at home!" her brother said appreciatively.

"That chicken we finished was no more delicious than yours, either!" David added.

"Now, you two had better watch your extravagant words, or I'll start to believe you!" Penny replied, laughing. Mrs. Daring had trained her daughter to be an excellent cook, like herself, and the boys never failed to express their appreciation—especially for Penny's desserts.

Mr. Daring then began to tell them about the history of the famous city they were visiting. "Marseille was founded in the sixth century before Christ by a colonizing force of Greeks from Asia Minor. The Greek city-states founded colonies all over the Mediterranean as bases for their trading enterprises, and this one was destined to become France's most important port. The Greek colonists built a fine harbor facility in the place they call the Old Port today, and parts of it are still there."

"This was a strategic spot," Mr. Daring continued, "because of its fine sheltered port and its key position on the great coastal road that led to Spain and Britain. Later, when Greek power declined, the city was incorporated into the growing Roman Empire. In 117 A.D. it was connected to Rome by the great highway, named the Via Aurelia, after the Emperor Aurelian. Rome's legions marched from Italy to the English channel along highways like that one."

He looked at his daughter with a twinkle in his eye. "In fact, young lady, we'll give you and the boys some great opportunities for pictures of ancient Roman ruins when we drive to Arles day after tomorrow!"

"But when will we get to Carcassone?" Mark asked. The boys were itching to see that ancient French city, with its two sets of fortified walls surrounding the historic stone towers.

"The next day, right after the trip to Arles, Mark," his father said with a laugh.

"I think he's worried about finding pastries on the way, Dad," Penny suggested with a straight face. "Remember, we only got him out of Paris by promising to feed him chocolates in Carcassone. Tell him he'll be O.K. if he has to wait another day to get there."

"I'm not thinking about chocolate," Mark insisted. "I'm thinking of those stone walls! Imagine, two complete walls, built so many centuries ago, still circling a city in the twentieth century! That place withstood sieges from all kinds of armies! We'll be walking in the middle of history!"

"Well, there's a lot to see here in Marseille," Mrs. Daring reminded them. "We'll see some of it tomorrow." Almost as tall as her daughter, Carolyn Daring was responsible for her children's learning the French language and culture. She'd started them at an early age, with songs and stories, then taught them the language using several cassette tape courses and the short wave radio. Now, as visitors to France, Mark and Penny were greatly enjoying their ability to understand what they heard and read, as well as their capacity to speak to people they encountered. David's family had taught him German, not French, so he was dependent on the Darings to translate for him on this trip.

The next day they spent the morning walking along the broad tree-shaded La Canebière that ran from the Old Port right through downtown Marseille. As they sauntered past the scores of shops and hotels and restaurants, Mrs. Daring told them the origin of the street's name.

"It's from the word *cannabis* which means hemp," she explained. "Sailing ships required endless amounts of strong rope, hemp, to hold up their masts, to raise and lower their sails, to lift small boats and cargo. Marseille was a great supplier of hemp to the sailing ships of ancient times. We can take a boat tour of the harbor and see the original Greek port, then we can visit the larger Roman area." Her eyes gleamed with pleasure at the prospect.

"The history of this place is fascinating," her husband added. "In the Middle Ages, Marseille was a major port for the expeditions that left for the Crusades. Thousands of soldiers set sail from here to fight in the Holy Land against the Mohammedans."

"And I just read in the guide book that headquarters for the French Foreign Legion is at an old church in town," David said. He and Mark were both intrigued by the military history of the area and had been reading all they could about this.

They wandered along the shady tree-lined boulevard, visiting shops, taking pictures, watching people from every part of the world stroll by. Later they lunched on the second-floor balcony of a restaurant that overlooked the fishing boats in the harbor.

None of them had noticed the two men who'd followed them all morning. The agents had taken turns keeping the Americans in sight, relieving each other periodically so that neither of them would be seen by their quarry too frequently.

After lunch the Americans joined a tour boat and were taken past scores of fishing boats and cruise vessels in the Old Port. Penny and the boys took pictures under a very bright blue sky. Many boats passed them, filled with other tourists or fishermen, and the white spray of their wakes shone brilliantly against the beautiful blue water. Gulls circled noisily overhead, feeding on scraps tossed from the boats.

That evening they enjoyed a marvelous feast of sea food at another restaurant along the Canebière. Here too they were followed, but they never saw those who were shadowing them.

Sergei and Uri had stayed well away from the Americans. Sergei knew that David had sensed his interest in the attack on Penny's camera case, so he took no chances of alerting the Americans again. He and Uri sat in a restaurant near the harbor, several blocks away from the wide boulevard where David and the Darings were sightseeing. Other agents kept the Americans in view.

Sergei spoke again of the failed attempt to steal the camera case from the American girl.

"They've got to think it was just a thief," Sergei reminded Uri.

Uri, slouched deep in his chair, was disturbed. A stocky, impatient man, he was visibly chafing under Sergei's restrictions.

"Why don't we just jump those stupid kids when they're staring at the shop windows?" he asked impatiently. "We could do it in a crowd and get away easily."

"We're not here to get caught!" Sergei snapped. When would this stupid thug learn the finer points of espionage? Always a bully, Uri thought only of force. *Uri has no patience*, Sergei realized with disgust. But he, Sergei, was a patient man, which was why he was boss of this team.

"We'll get our chance," he said confidently. "The others are keeping an eye on them so we don't have to risk being seen again. I know that boy was suspicious of me and we would be fools to expose ourselves again."

He looked directly at Uri. "Remember, we lost that letter once. We'll never get it back if we let ourselves be arrested!"

Uri sighed. He had to do what he was told—at least for now.

CHAPTER 4

THE WALLED CITY OF CARCASSONE

While Mr. and Mrs. Daring lingered at the museum, the young people went on a walking tour through the city's old streets. They'd seen Carcassone first the night before as they drove their rented car from Marseille. Brilliantly lit, shining like a magic city from legendary times, the tall pointed towers above the walls accented the ancient fortifications which had withstood attacks and sieges throughout the centuries. The town was shaped like an ellipse, and the two sets of fortified walls, one within the other, enclosed houses, churches, the cathedral, and the castle. Within the walls also were many shops for the tourist trade, some of them elegant, most not.

The Darings had taken rooms in a hotel in the newer part of the city across the river from the old fortified town. All of them had slept well after their long drive and were now reveling in the remarkable sights around them.

"Did you know that the Emperor Charlemagne

besieged this city for five years, but it never surrendered?" David asked Penny and Mark as they strolled along. "In fact, he couldn't even starve the people into surrendering!" David and Mark devoured the guidebooks and histories they found in their travels. "Every summer he attacked," David continued, "but each time the city's soldiers beat him back."

"Well, if he'd had some hang gliders and specially trained troops, they could have sailed in by night, captured the city's gate, and opened it for his army," Mark replied with the knowing air of a military strategist.

"Mark, that's a brilliant idea!" Penny said. "Why didn't you tell him that—back in the ninth century—when he was trying to capture the place?"

"He didn't ask me," Mark answered simply. "I wanted to tell him how to take cities, but he didn't ask me. No wonder he never captured the place!"

Penny rolled her eyes at David, marveling at her brother's foolish claim, and the three moved upward along the narrow winding streets between the stone buildings. She'd been taking photographs since they'd entered the old city after breakfast that morning.

"This is the most fascinating place I've ever seen!" she exclaimed, brown eyes shining. "Imagine! We're actually walking in a city built in the *Middle Ages*!"

"There's a restaurant, Penny," David observed suddenly. "We'd better stop and let Mark tank up before he collapses. After all, we promised him chocolates and pastries in Carcassone. I'm not hungry myself, but, as Christians, we have to keep our promise even to a glutton!"

"I guess you're right, David," she agreed solemnly. "We'd better stop. It's a pity really, I mean, to have to stop seeing these historical places just to watch a food addict gorge himself again!" She wore her plaid skirt with matching headband, which David liked so much.

"O.K., folks," Mark said in his matter-of-fact way, "I realize I have no right to pull you from your historical studies." He slapped his hand against his forehead. "How selfish I've been! And how noble and self-sacrificing you two are! How could I be so mean?"

He staggered to a stop in the narrow lane, leaned against an ancient wall, and looked distressed at his self-centered attitude. Shaking his head, he said, "I repent! I really do. I won't make you stop any more. Just go on and soak up history while I pause here for some chocolate éclairs!"

"We can't leave him, Penny," David said, ignoring Mark's plea. "We're obligated. I mean, *someone* has to stay with him and lead him home after he's stuffed himself. We've got to sacrifice our own wishes so we can take care of the poor addict."

"You're right, David," she agreed, sitting down at a cafe table while the boys sat on either side. "And I admire your nobility for being willing to look after him all the time like this. You inspire me to put up with him a little longer." She sighed a sigh of dutiful heroism as she put her camera case on the table before her, opened it, and took out her Olympus.

The waiter, a tall man in black suit with white apron, arrived in a few minutes, and Penny, speaking fluent French, ordered chocolate pastries for herself and David. David knew German but not French so he had to rely completely on Penny and Mark to order his food in France. Mark ordered for himself, and they continued their banter until the treats were served.

"How did they live in this city for so long when armies surrounded it?" Penny asked seriously as they ate. "Wouldn't they run out of food and water?"

"They stored food by the ton," David answered. "And they stored hundreds of barrels of water; they also had a huge cistern. In fact, by the fourteenth century, a cistern in the Narbonne Tower could hold enough water for the whole city for six months! And they had a mill for grinding the wheat they'd stored, and blacksmiths to make armor and arrows. It was incredible what they could make and store."

Across the narrow lane, leaning in the shadow of a shop doorway, a tall man in dark shirt and trousers watched the three Americans. Lean and muscular, Louis wore a blue beret angled across his eyes, had a thick moustache, and seemed to have nothing better to do than whittle a stick with a long knife as he held up the wall with his shoulder. A cigarette drooped from his thin lips and a light-colored scar ran across his left cheek. He handled the knife with great skill.

Louis watched the taller boy get up, leave the other two teenagers at the table, cross the street, and enter one of the shops. The blond boy stayed with the girl, however. In fact, the man had noticed, one of the boys was *always* with her; she was never alone in the streets or in a shop. He cursed the care those boys took to guard Penny wherever they went.

It doesn't make my job any easier if she's the target, Louis thought as he whittled and watched. *But those American punks can't stop a real fighting man*, he concluded. It just made the job longer, and that irritated him. It also irritated him to be pulled off his assignment in the Riviera to trail teenage Americans. He hadn't yet been told exactly what he was to do; only that he would be joined later in the day and would receive precise instructions at that time.

In a few minutes the taller boy came back into sight and sat again at the table, handing the girl what Louis guessed was a package of film for her camera.

Louis kept his eyes on the three, and saw an older couple, obviously their parents, join them. After a few minutes, they all got up and continued their walk through the city. Louis sauntered after them at some distance, strolling idly, whittling, and smoking as he moved among the people in the narrow streets, always keeping the Americans in sight.

They stopped frequently to take photographs. The girl was a serious craftsman, he noted, framing each shot with studious care. The boys had smaller cameras, used them less frequently, yet more quickly. Louis filed away such details as he followed the family up a sloping narrow lane, weaving among tourists, pausing when his quarry did, taking care not to be noticed. These people were so dumb they'd never see someone following them! Louis yawned with the boredom of this assignment.

Then he stiffened. The father had looked briefly at him and then looked away, apparently noticing nothing but the scenery. But several minutes later, the stocky blond boy happened to turn and look in his direction also. The boy's glance swept the area and didn't stop at Louis. But had the father told him to look back? Could they actually be keeping watch?

Suddenly Louis felt uneasy. And he was a professional who knew when to follow his instincts. Instantly he turned into a shop on his left, taking himself completely out of their sight. They couldn't get away from him in that lane anyway.

Now he was very alert, his boredom gone. He'd been ordered to follow the Americans without being noticed, and this had proved such a simple task that he'd been caught off guard when the men looked back at him. Had they suspected what he was doing?

Walking back into the shop, Louis stepped to the counter and asked the proprietor for a phone. "None!" the man said sharply. He'd have to use the public one down at the intersection. Fuming, Louis realized he would have to wait a while before stepping out of the door into the street. He knew that he had to inform his boss that the Americans might be watching for trouble. This added a whole new dimension to the situation. His boss hadn't figured that the Americans were keeping watch, or that they suspected anything. Sweating with the realization that he might have blundered, Louis stood inside the shop, wondering when it would be safe to look outside.

He waited several minutes before stepping cautiously into the narrow street. Looking casually in the direction the Americans had gone, he failed to see any of them. He began walking that way, looking into stores as he passed, seeming in no hurry, yet rather anxious, now that his quarry was not in sight. He passed a number of stores, glancing briefly into each as he did so, knowing that such quick glances could easily miss the people he sought.

He was really sweating now, trying not to picture his boss's response if he lost the people he'd been sent to follow. He cursed himself for his carelessness. He'd broken a vital rule of his trade: never take a situation for granted, never relax, not ever.

Anxiously he came to a narrow intersection where a road slanted in from the left, crossed the one he was on, then slanted off to his right. Which way should he go?

Behind him, Mark flipped the switch of his camera, activating the telephoto lens. Just inside a shop door, he could barely see Louis's face through the crowd as the man looked up the street to his left. When a gap in the crowd appeared, Mark took a quick picture, and another, then stepped back into the store.

Mr. Daring had taken his wife, Penny, and David into a leather shop, where he directed their attention to the marvelous leather purses. Neither of the ladies had heard him tell Mark and David of the man who followed them, nor had they heard him suggest that Mark try to get the man's picture after he'd passed the shop.

Stuffing his camera back into his trousers' pocket, Mark joined David who was examining leather belts on the counter. David looked inquiringly at him, and Mark nodded slightly and grinned. "Got him," he said quietly.

They stayed in the shop for another ten minutes before Mr. Daring led them outside. The sun's light was dazzling after the darkness of the shop's interior, and they all blinked as their eyes adjusted to the change. Daring and the boys looked along the narrow street in both directions, but didn't spot the man they'd suspected of following them.

"Maybe he was just a tourist like us," Mark suggested quietly to his father while his mother and Penny looked up the street.

"Maybe he was, Mark," Daring replied. "But it pays to keep our eyes open. And we can send that picture to Henri, in Paris, just in case. Since we left Egypt two weeks ago, there have been too many strange things happening for us to let down our guard now." He grinned at his son. "So let's keep our eyes open, and these precious girls safe! That's our job!"

"Yes, sir!" Mark replied. Both he and David had been trained by their fathers in self-defense. Both had been taught their responsibility as men for the safety of women and girls.

Later that evening they sat in the hotel restaurant. They'd enjoyed another magnificent French meal, and Jim Daring and his wife were sipping strong coffee while the youngsters ate dessert. The men had seen no further sign of the man they had suspected of following them, and Mark and David were prepared to believe that he was just another tourist.

Jim Daring was not convinced. While waiting for his wife and Penny to join them in the hotel lobby, he'd told the boys about his phone call to Henri in Paris. "I also told him of the attempt to steal Penny's camera case at the train station. We both agreed it could have been just one of the many thieves who abound in this city; but Henri urged me to remind you two that we should all keep alert."

Carolyn Daring and Penny had joined them then, and they had gone into the hotel restaurant. Now, after dinner, they were all relaxed.

"There's street dancing in the old town tonight," Mr. Daring said to his wife as they sipped their coffee. "Would you like to go, sweetheart?"

"What about tomorrow night?" she asked. "You boys wore me out today! After our long walk and this meal, I probably have enough energy for a short stroll before bed, but not much else! And I'd really like to finish these letters I started."

"That's fine with me," he replied.

"Can we go to the street dance, Dad?" Penny asked eagerly. She'd been looking forward to this ever since she'd read about this custom in Carcassone.

"Let's all go together tomorrow, Penny," her father replied. "The boys will be just as eager tomorrow, I think." He grinned at Mark, but especially at David.

"We sure will," Mark replied.

David's face got red.

"Oh, Mark," his mother said, "I forgot my post-cards. I could write some of them while I enjoy the rest of this coffee. Would you mind going up to the room and getting them for me?"

"Sure, Mom," Mark replied, rising and heading for the stairs. He ignored the elevator as often as he could. He and David had not had their regular exercise since arriving in France, and he craved some bodily action.

As he hurried toward the stairs, Mark failed to see the consternation on the face of a tall man standing in the hall. White-faced, the watching man hurried to a phone in the lobby and dialed frantically.

But the tall man was too late.

CHAPTER 5

THE MAID WITH THE CAMERA CASE

Mark raced up the stairs, moved quickly through the door into the hall, and pulled the key from his pocket with one hand while he turned the doorknob with the other. It was unlocked!

Puzzled, he opened the door and stepped inside—just as the phone began to ring. To his great surprise he faced a maid, who was holding the phone in one hand, and Penny's camera case in the other. She looked at him in alarm and put down the phone in a hurry.

"Hey!" Mark called, moving quickly toward her. "Give me that!"

She handed the camera case to him with an anguished look and burst into a torrent of frantic explanations in French. She spoke so quickly that Mark could barely follow her meaning, as she tried to persuade him that she'd been preparing their beds for the night when her supervisor called to give her more

30

instructions. Hastily she backed toward the hall, right out of the room, and closed the door behind her.

Mark was stunned. He knew that in Europe the employees came into your room at various times to clean, and even to turn down the bed covers at night. But what was she doing with Penny's camera case?

He searched the case. The camera was there, with two lenses and some boxes of film. Curiously, he looked in the outer pocket on the side of the case. Here he found a foreign-looking envelope. Turning it over, he saw it had no writing on it—yet it was sealed. Feeling carefully with his fingers, however, he could tell that there was paper inside.

He looked around the room which Penny shared with their parents, but he couldn't see anything out of the ordinary. Nothing seemed disturbed; although, as he looked closer, he noticed that Penny had left her suitcase open. *That's curious*, he thought, *not like Penny at all*. She took meticulous care of her possessions, and did not leave things open. *And why would the maid be holding Penny's camera case when the phone rang? And who would be calling?*

Mark went to the dresser, found the postcards his mother had requested, and left the room, taking the camera case with him. As he locked the door behind him, he realized that any employee who had a master key could get in.

A puzzled frown wreathed Mark's friendly face as he walked into the dining room and rejoined his family.

After placing the camera case on the table in front of Penny, he gave the cards to his mother. Then he told them what he'd found when he entered their room.

"What would she be doing with my camera case?" Penny asked in alarm.

"Maybe she was just moving it from the bed when the phone rang," David suggested.

"But I didn't leave it on the bed," Penny replied, "I left it shut up in my suitcase, just as you said to do, Dad."

"Your suitcase was open when I walked in the room," Mark said quietly. "The maid must have opened it."

This news stunned them all. Jim Daring's face was solemn. "I'll talk to the manager," he said, rising. "Have some more coffee, Carolyn; I won't be long."

He came back in a few minutes, stood by their table, and spoke quietly. "The manager said that no maid had been sent to our room since this afternoon. He wants you to come to the lobby, Mark, and see if you can identify the woman you saw. You folks stay here."

Mark followed his father to the lobby. Here the manager, a Monsieur Dupré, stood waiting. Of middle age, smartly dressed in a dark blue suit, his long face showed his distress. Mr. Daring introduced Mark to him, and, in English, Monsieur Dupré told them how he wished to handle this.

"Let me lead you on a tour of the hotel's ground floor, and you look at the employees as we go through the kitchen and the offices. If you recognize the woman you saw, don't say anything at that time; wait until we've left the room, then tell me."

He led them first to the kitchen, pointing with obvious pride to the chefs, the tables, the ovens where the food was prepared, and the refrigeration rooms. Then he led them to the utility rooms, to the laundry, to smaller and larger areas on the first floor of the hotel, and to the offices.

As they left each room, Monsieur Dupré looked inquiringly at Mark. But Mark always shook his head. "None of those," he said.

And that was how it ended. "You've seen all the maids," Monsieur Dupré told him when they returned to the lobby and stood in a corner, out of the hearing of the woman at the desk.

"None of them was the one in our room," Mark said emphatically. "She was short, about middle aged, and had dark hair. She dressed like the other maids, but she wasn't among those that you showed me."

Monsieur Dupré was most apologetic. "Then some woman who impersonated my maid was in your room, Mr. Daring. This is most distressing. Have you lost anything?"

"Not that we know of," Daring replied. "We'll check. My daughter insists that she left her camera case shut up in her suitcase. And yet Mark took it from the maid, or the woman posing as the maid. We'll look into all our things and let you know at once if we think anything's gone."

Mark and his father returned to the dining room

and rejoined Mrs. Daring, Penny, and David. Jim Daring's face was thoughtful as he described the results of their tour with Monsieur Dupré. He spoke quietly so as not to be heard by the people at the adjoining table.

"Mark didn't recognize the woman he'd seen in our room, and Monsieur Dupré said he'd shown him all the maids who worked on this shift."

That's when Mark took the envelope out of his pocket and handed it to his sister. "Is this yours, Penny?"

She took it from his hand with a puzzled look, turned it over, and shook her head. "Nope, I've never seen it. Where'd you get it?"

"From the outside pocket of your camera case," he replied. "It was stuck down inside."

"But how did it get there?" she asked, handing the letter to her father.

"Could there be a connection between the thief who tried to take her camera case at the train station, and the woman acting as a maid, and the letter?" Carolyn Daring asked her husband.

"Could be, Carolyn," he replied, looking thoughtfully at her for a moment. He'd often thought his wife had the instincts of a detective in the way she searched for causes and connections. Then he turned the letter over in his hand and examined it again. Taking out his pocket knife he slit it open, and took out a single sheet of paper. Both sides were covered with typing.

"What does it say, Dad?" Penny asked eagerly, leaning forward.

"It's a list of names," her father answered. "Here, Carolyn, your French is better than mine. I can read the names, but not all the titles and descriptions." He handed the letter to his wife.

Two blocks away from the hotel, a short woman in black servant's dress ducked into a parked car whose back door opened just as she arrived. Immediately the car pulled out from the curb and moved rapidly along the street before turning to the right and speeding away. Inside, the weeping woman explained to the angry man beside the driver that she'd just had time to find the camera case before her companion called from the lobby to warn her that the young American was coming to his parents' room. She was on the phone when the boy walked in!

Sergei was incensed. "How close we came! How did that young man know to return to the room just then?"

"I don't think he knew anything," the driver said. "I saw his father hand him the keys to their room, and he just walked up the stairs before I could warn Olga of his coming. The rest of the family stayed at their table, so he must have gone to get something for them."

Sergei had a sick feeling in his stomach. Nothing had gone right on this mission, not since they'd let that hostage rejoin his mother in Paris. They'd released her son on the condition that she give them that letter with its damaging list of names. But she'd stuck it in the camera case of the American girl sitting beside her in the restaurant, she'd said—and the American girl had left the restaurant and taken a taxi before Sergei could catch her! Since then, they'd been desperately trying to get that camera case back and retrieve the letter inside, before it ended up in the hands of the police.

"Did that young man seem suspicious when he found you in the room?" Sergei asked the weeping woman.

"Yes," she replied, her voice stretched thin with fear, "he did! He demanded the camera case at once. I made an excuse, but I'm sure he saw the open suitcase where I'd found the case. It took several minutes for me to find it, or I would have been out of the room when he came." She dabbed her eyes with her handkerchief, sick with anxiety at what would happen to her because of her failure.

"We didn't have much time for Olga to impersonate a maid and get into that room, Sergei" the driver reminded the tall Russian. "We just couldn't put this together that fast. It almost worked, though." He thought that it might have been very much worse. "I'm glad Olga got out without being arrested!" he reminded Sergei.

Sergei came to his senses. He had to restore these people's morale. "You are certainly right," he responded. "Olga, it was amazing that you could have stolen that dress in the hotel and gotten the key as you did! I will put that in my report most emphatically."

She wept with relief.

Inwardly, however, Sergei cursed them for their failure. It was *his* neck that was in real danger. But he had to keep them loyal, because he didn't know how much help he'd get from Paris. These two could witness to his own great efforts, and they could testify to the impossibility of their achieving success in such a short time.

Time! That was the problem! They had needed more time to do this job. But they hadn't been given enough time.

Sergei looked through the window at the darkened countryside flashing past, and his thoughts were bleak. What would those Americans be thinking now? What would they be doing? Surely they knew now that the camera case was important to someone other than themselves.

CHAPTER 6

"WE'VE GOT TO GET HELP!"

"We've got to get help," Mr. Daring said.

They'd returned to their room, searched carefully, but found no sign of anything missing or otherwise disturbed. Mrs. Daring and Penny sat on the large bed, while Jim Daring and David sat in chairs beside the dresser. Mark leaned against the wall facing the ladies.

"Whom can we call, Jim?" his wife asked. She was now truly alarmed at the two incidents involving Penny's camera case, and the news from her husband that he and Mark had spotted a man following them that day as they toured the city.

"I'll call Henri, in Paris," he said decisively. "He's the one who helped us out when that gang jumped the kids in the catacombs, and he'll tell us what to do now."

He picked up the letter and looked again at the names. "This is a list of people in government departments, in two universities in Paris, in two banks, and several editorial positions in newspapers and magazines and television. All the names are French.

Obviously, this list is important! I think that's the reason that thief tried to get it in Marseille, and why we were followed in town, and why that woman dressed as a maid took Penny's case out of her suitcase. She almost got away with it, until the phone rang to warn her that Mark was on the way to the room."

"That was a close one, Dad!" Mark exclaimed. "If Mom hadn't asked me to get those postcards, I wouldn't have gone to the room, and the woman would have gotten away with the letter."

"But who put it in Penny's case in the first place?" her mother asked. "And why?"

"I bet someone did it to hide it from someone else," Penny answered thoughtfully. "They must have thought that they could get it back. Wonder where they did it, though? I've always got my camera with me."

"We've got to get rid of this letter!" Daring stated firmly. "As long as we've got it, someone will try to get it from us."

"Or as long as someone *thinks* that we have it," David suggested. "If they think we have it, they'll keep trying to get it."

Daring looked at him for a minute, then glanced thoughtfully over at his wife. "David's right," he replied slowly. "Even if we get rid of the letter, we'll still be in danger—as long as the people trying to get it think it's in our hands!"

"Oh, Jim," his wife asked, "how can we get our children in such situations?"

"I don't know, honey, but we've got to get *out* of this one at once! I'll call Henri right away." He got up and walked to the bedside table where the telephone rested.

"Mr. Daring," David asked suddenly, "how can we be sure the wrong people aren't listening to our phone?"

Daring halted and pondered this point.

Mark thought of something else. "Dad, the people on that list are placed in some very influential positions in government, in the media, in finance, and the universities. They must have powerful friends who don't want their names exposed—at least, not on that list, all together like that."

"That makes sense, Mark," his father replied thoughtfully. He stood for a moment thinking; how *could* they reach Henri in Paris, without being overheard?

"If anyone's listening to our call," David asked, "will they know Henri's connection with French intelligence?"

"Yes," Daring replied, "they will. I have the numbers for his office and his home phone. Anyone with connections in intelligence or police will know very quickly that he's with French customs and counter intelligence."

This sobered them all. How could they reach Henri without alerting their pursuers?

"Let's do this for now," Daring decided finally, crossing the room to the desk against the wall. "I'll copy this list twice, and we can mail one to Henri tomorrow. We'll also call him from an outside phone."

"Then we can't call him until tomorrow?" his wife asked.

"I don't see how," her husband answered, "not from the hotel."

"Dad, no one knows for sure that we've found this letter," Mark said.

"They might suspect we're wondering why the maid had the camera case in her hand, though," Penny said.

"But they won't know for sure, will they? We probably have time, certainly until tomorrow," Mark replied.

"I think you're right, Mark," his father said, as he took his correspondence case from the bedside table and turned to his daughter. "Help me out, Penny. You make one copy while I make another." He gave her a sheet of paper and a pen.

She joined him at the table as Mark brought a chair across the room and placed it beside the one his father had taken. Carolyn Daring and the boys were silent as the two copied the names from the letter. When they'd finished, Daring took out three envelopes, his business stationery, actually, with his home address in Africa, and placed the letters in them.

"I'll write a cover letter to Henri in two of these," he said. "Then we can ask the manager to put the original in his safe."

"Sir," David suggested, "would it be worthwhile to let someone steal Penny's case, without the camera and lens, of course! I mean, if they took the case and found the letter, wouldn't that satisfy them for a while?"

"David, that's a good suggestion!" Daring replied. He pondered this a moment.

"But Dad, I love this case!" Penny said, a frown on her face. "You gave it to me two years ago, and I've taken it everywhere!"

"Honey, it might be safe anyway," her father replied, "if we could leave it where someone could look through it without having to take the whole thing. All they want is the letter. If they get that, they'll probably be satisfied."

"If they don't have to steal the whole thing to make it look like robbery," his wife added.

"But won't they suspect something's wrong if they find the letter's been opened?" Penny insisted. "They can see that you cut the envelope open, Daddy."

"They might," Daring agreed, "they might. But they might realize that we can't be expected to know what the names mean or have any reason to do anything about it. The more I think about this, the better it sounds."

"Well, they might also suspect that whoever put the letter there had cut it open. They don't necessarily have to think it was us," Carolyn Daring said to her husband.

"You're right!" he replied with an affectionate smile. "I said you thought like a detective!"

"Daddy, I know this is serious," Penny said. "I can always get another camera case—so do whatever you think is best." She smiled.

"I'll buy you another if you have to sacrifice this

one, Penny." Her dad smiled back.

So that's how they left it. The original letter was put back into its envelope in the open pocket of Penny's case. Mr. Daring addressed one of the other envelopes and put a copy inside. "I'll mail this tomorrow from the city post office, along with all our postcards. And tomorrow I'll find a safe phone and read the other copy to Henri. Then we can think of a way to let someone find Penny's camera case and search it for the letter. How's that?"

They all agreed that this plan was a good one.

"Let's ask the Lord to give us wisdom to handle this situation properly," Mr. Daring said, taking out his Bible. He began to read from Genesis 32, commenting on the prudence with which Jacob made his preparations to meet his vengeful brother, as well as on his prayer and total dependence on God for protection. "That's all we can do ourselves," he said. "Pray for wisdom; then do what seems wise."

The family prayed together at day's end.

CHAPTER 7

"THIS IS DISASTER!"

"This is disaster!" Schmidt's raspy voice barked into the phone.

Sergei winced. The conversation had not gone well. Yet he hadn't been blamed, which was a real surprise, since the people he worked for always looked for scapegoats when their operations failed.

"Not necessarily, sir," Sergei replied. "The Darings are still in the hotel. We don't know that they've found the letter. And what would they do with it if they did?"

"Plenty! We know more about that family now than we did when you left Paris," the scratchy voice answered. "Jim Daring is a mining engineer, and he's working on a top secret project for the Egyptian government. He's working with a French-German company that has high connections in the French government, and he's got contacts in their intelligence community."

This is getting worse all the time, Sergei thought, sick at heart.

"It's still possible," he suggested, trying to sound respectful, "that they haven't found the letter. Olga said that the girl keeps her film inside the case. She probably never looks in that outside pocket. We've still got a chance, I think."

There was silence from the other end. Sergei waited nervously, as he sat in the dingy hotel room he and Uri had taken, not far from the hotel where the Darings stayed. He'd sent Uri out while he made this call.

"When can you try again?" the gravelly voice asked finally.

"We can actually grab the girl and rip away the case and her purse. It would look like robbery, pure and simple. Uri is itching to get into action," he added.

"You watch Uri!" Schmidt insisted. "That's why we put you in charge of this, Sergei, and not him! The fool thinks only of physical force; he has no finesse."

"Yes, sir," Sergei replied, "but this may be the time for force. Not violence," he hastened to add, "but force—just taking that case away from the girl."

"How can you do this?"

"We can manage it in crowds of tourists," Sergei said. "We'll find a place where we can escape, and block out the father and those two boys—they never leave their mother and daughter unattended! But we can do it."

"Don't do anything to bring in the police. That's the very thing we're trying to avoid."

"Yes, sir," Sergei replied.

The rasping voice sighed in deep frustration. *The man sounded very tired*, Sergei thought in surprise. "Go ahead, then," Schmidt said. "Grab that girl and get the letter. The KGB can't afford to lose this network in Paris. The western media tried to persuade their peoples that we were out of business with the fall of the Soviet Empire, and for a while that's what people believed. But now, with our communist strength in the new Russian parliament, people know that our activities have actually increased! And if our vital Paris network is exposed, there'll be a terrible outcry—even the American media won't be able to conceal it. And then we'll face a cutoff of the western aid and money we need so desperately! You're our last hope of getting that list and avoiding disaster!"

Then he added, "You had asked for more help with that hostage in Paris, hadn't you?"

"Yes, sir," Sergei said, his heart leaping. Maybe he wouldn't get blamed for that either. "We were too shorthanded. That woman in Paris refused flatly to hand over the letter without seeing her son. We don't have the team we used to, and I just didn't have enough people to handle it properly."

He paused, then realized he'd better be more diplomatic. You *never ever* implied that your superiors were at fault, *in any way*. "But it was my responsibility, sir," he said carefully. "I should have found a way." That was tough to admit.

There was a silence. Then the voice spoke again.

"Well, we can only do the best we can. I know you have."

Sergei was astounded at this admission. He could only gulp and answer, "Thank you, sir."

The line went dead. Sergei sat on his bed in the small room, pondering. His boss had never shown such understanding of a failed mission before. Nor had he sounded so tired—defeated almost.

But Schmidt would not give up, Sergei realized. His boss meant to do all he could to maintain the espionage network that had served the Communist Empire so well and terrorized the world for the past fifty years. And Sergei would do his part; he wouldn't give up either. He put his mind to recovering that letter from the Darings.

The next morning, Jim Daring and David left the hotel early, walked quickly down the stairs, and strode along the street to the post office. Entering this building they walked over to the row of public phones against the wall. Daring picked up a receiver, listened for the tone, then put the instrument down, and picked up another.

"It's dead," he said to David, who stood beside him to see that no one got too close while Daring read the names from the list to Henri in Paris.

Twice more he tried. Finally, the fourth phone worked. He placed the call, and waited—and waited.

"No answer, David," he said. "I'll call his office and leave a message." He tried the other number.

"No one's there," he said with a shrug. "We'll have to call later. We can at least mail the letter."

A man entered the post office and approached the phones. Daring and David ignored him and walked casually over to the window. As the man behind them placed his call and began to talk, Daring said quietly to David: "We'll wait till he leaves before we mail the letter. No sense advertising what we're doing."

The man at the phone spoke for only a few minutes and then left. Daring at once walked to the mail slots and threw in the letter to Henri, along with a half dozen postcards.

"Let's go!" he grinned at David. Vastly relieved at being able to deposit the letter, they left the building and walked rapidly back to the hotel.

"Am I happy to get that letter off!" Daring remarked as they walked along the sidewalk. "At least Henri will have that in a couple of days and can take action on it. Now, all we have to do is somehow let those guys—whoever they are—rummage through Penny's camera case, find the letter, and bug off!"

"Where should we leave it so they can find it?" David asked.

"I guess our room's the only place. They might or might not try to get in there again. Monsieur Dupré most definitely doesn't want police hanging around, and since we told him nothing was stolen, he probably won't have the place watched. Those guys could send someone else into our room as soon as they learn we'll be gone all morning. I'll announce that loudly at the desk as we leave," he grinned.

The two stepped from the curb and crossed the street. Daring continued, "If we left her case in a public place, it'd be taken by common thieves. Those guys chasing the letter are the only ones who want it bad enough to get into the hotel room again."

He shook his head as they walked briskly along. "What a mess! Penny and Mark say you're the one who's drawn all this danger, David!" He looked with mock seriousness at the young man in slacks and dark shirt beside him. "What do you think? Are you responsible for all this action in their normally peaceful lives?"

David laughed. "Well, sir, they accuse me of this all the time. But I keep telling them I'm the scholarly type; I'm a reader. I never got involved in such things until I came to visit them! Actually, the more you examine all the evidence, the more obvious it is that they're the ones drawing *me* into all this trouble!"

Jim Daring laughed and clapped him on the shoulder as they entered the hotel. They took the stairs, reached their floor, and strode to the room. Daring knocked. There was no reply.

"Maybe they went down to breakfast," he suggested to David, as he took out his key and unlocked the door. They entered.

"Look! The camera case is gone!" David said.

Daring turned to Penny's bed against the wall to their left. "You're right, David," he replied. "She said she'd leave it there when they went down to the restaurant. It didn't take those people—whoever they are—long to get in and steal it!"

They searched the room, but found no evidence that anything else had been disturbed.

Daring smiled at David. "Maybe your plan worked!"

"I sure hope so!" David replied.

"Let's join the others for some breakfast," Daring said.

Later that morning they were driving their rental car back to the old city.

"Well, Dad, David's plan worked, but I still need a camera case," Penny said. "Don't you think he should be the one to buy me one? After all, it was his idea." Penny sat in back, squashed between the two boys in the small auto.

"Let's think about that," her father replied, laughing.

"I've been thinking about it," David said, "and it seems to me that Penny's sacrifice for all of us is such a noble deed, we'd actually be insulting her if we offered to pay for it. I know she'd refuse."

"David's right, Dad," Mark added. "You can't *insult* people when they're generous like that. And Penny's been so generous that it would be cruel for anyone to offer money for her sacrifice."

Penny tried to reply but David beat her to it. "It'd actually make it look like she was doing it to get herself a new case. And that wouldn't be fair to her."

"Wait a minute!" Penny protested. "All this talk

about sacrifice is true, of course. But Dad still promised to get me another case if mine was stolen. And I just thought that David, who's been eating us out of house and home these past three weeks, and costing us all kinds of money—I just thought that he'd be generous enough to repay Dad in this small way."

She tossed her head, still trying to keep a straight face. "I overestimated his nobility and generosity."

"Well, of course I'm grateful, Penny," David insisted. "But I'm too noble even to—"

"*I'll* buy you a new case, Penny!" her father interrupted with a laugh. "I promised I would, and I will."

"Well, it's a relief to know that those people have finally got what they want," Carolyn Daring said, changing the subject. "I just hope that getting that letter back satisfies them. Maybe now we can live in peace."

"I think we can relax now, Carolyn," her husband assured her. "David and I mailed that list to Henri. He's not in his office apparently, but I'll call again when we get back this afternoon. At least that list is in the mail. Henri will soon get it to the right people."

"I wonder about those names, Dad," Penny said. "They were highly placed people, weren't they?"

"They were, indeed. We'll ask Henri when we get back to Paris."

Weaving the rental car though the thickening traffic, Jim Daring found a parking place and pulled to a stop. "Let's look for some history now, and forget those names and thieves for a while!

CHAPTER 8

"THERE'S THAT MAN AGAIN!"

"Gosh! What a spectacular sight!" Mark exclaimed. The Daring family and David stood on the ancient walls of Carcassone and gazed at the snowcapped Pyrenées Mountains miles away to the east and south.

"The Pyrenées run for three hundred miles," his father told them, "and form a natural barrier between Spain and France. Archaeologists have found evidences of human settlement as far back as the sixth century before Christ. The Romans moved into the area around 50 B.C., and developed scores of mineral baths for their vacation spots. Even back in Roman times, rich citizens would come great distances to splash in the sulphur water. They thought it had healing powers."

"Look at the sunlight flash off the snow on the peaks," Penny observed. "How high are they, Dad?"

"Some of them are more than ten thousand feet high on the Spanish side. The French side is a bit lower. They really rival the Alps and have a booming skiing industry. It's quite a winter resort."

"How'd you like to try scaling these walls with people throwing spears and hot pitch down on you?" Mark asked, changing the subject abruptly as he looked down at the ground so far below them.

"I wouldn't like it a bit!" his mother replied.

They walked along the walls with other tourists, marveling at the ancient fortifications, the thickness of the walls, the openings or turrets for archers. They were on the inner walls, and could look down on the outer fortifications that also circled the city. Mr. and Mrs. Daring walked on ahead to look far into the green countryside.

Suddenly a woman behind them fell, crashing into Penny before falling to her knees. Penny stumbled, recovered her balance, and turned. Mark and David were already helping the flustered woman to her feet. David retrieved the woman's large black purse, as Mark steadied her.

Apologizing profusely to Penny for falling into her, she thanked the boys in what they took to be Italian. Assured that she was O.K., the three turned and resumed their stroll. Mr. and Mrs. Daring had not noticed the incident that delayed the kids.

Penny's face was grave. "Mark, I saw a man back there who looks like one of the men we saw in the train station."

Mark and David were instantly attentive. "Are you sure?" Mark asked, frowning. Neither he nor David looked back, not wanting to tip off the man who might be tailing them.

"Yes," she replied. "Not the tall man that stared at David, but the stocky one." Her voice showed that she was worried.

"Well, maybe he's just following to make sure we're out of the picture as far as that letter is concerned," her brother suggested. "They've got to know we're just tourists, down here to see the sights."

"Tell us what he looks like, Penny," David said.

"He's stocky, not tall like the other one. And he's wearing dark trousers and a dark shirt and a blue beret. He's got a cruel face," she added.

"Did he see that you'd noticed him?" Mark asked.

"I don't think so. He was watching you boys help the woman. Then he turned so you couldn't see him, and pretended to look back at the church steeple."

They walked along the narrow path between stone walls, moving from turret to turret with the other visitors. But now Penny was asking herself about the similarity of that man to the one at the Marseille train station.

"Maybe I just imagined this," she suggested. "Maybe he's not the same man at all."

"Well, Penny," David said, "you're a photographer, and you really notice things. Let's just act as if it's the same guy and keep our eyes open. He can't be doing anything but following us, because they've got your camera case."

"I think you're right," Mark added. "Maybe he didn't get the word from the one in charge and is still following us until he's called off. Let's just look carefully every once in a while and see if he stays with us."

The three of them caught up with Jim and Carolyn Daring and continued their tour. Periodically they would stop while one of them took a photograph. The walls were fascinating with towers of varying heights, and the whole defensive layout was intriguing, especially to Jim Daring and the boys.

At one end of the crescent-shaped city, they looked out over a steep bank below.

"Boy! I bet no one tried to attack the walls from that spot!" Mark said.

"You never know," his father replied. "All through history, great battles have been won, and major cities overthrown, when the attackers did what the defenders were sure they *wouldn't* do! Surprise is one of the key elements in war—and in many other human activities."

"That's what Dad told me to look for in reading military history," David told them. "That's a vital principle in war, he says, and in personal defense too. 'Do the unexpected!' he's told me."

"That's very true," Jim Daring agreed. "Sometimes, when you see that you're about to be attacked, it pays to attack first. When people think you won't do something, then that's the time to do it."

That night after dinner they all came back to the old town. Mr. and Mrs. Daring remained near the city gate, while Mark, Penny, and David walked on to see the street dancing. Penny wore a full dark-blue skirt

with white blouse, while the boys wore dark trousers
and sweaters.

"Keep your eyes open, and keep Penny safe,"
Daring reminded the boys as they left.

"Yes, sir," they repled.

"I'll be safe, Dad," Penny laughed. "They won't let
me go anywhere by myself. I'm practically a prisoner!
You'd think they were my guards and that I was a
famous spy or something!" She didn't look like this
made her too unhappy.

"That's fine," her father replied. "That's what I
want them to do."

The three wandered out toward the great open
square of the inner city among crowds of people from
all over the world. Bands were playing, and the
teenagers moved from spot to spot, watching folk in
various costumes. Gradually they worked their way
down the rue St. Louis toward the huge cathedral.

Here, too, crowds of people swirled in the lights that
threw the dancing shadows on the stone walls. The
three wound their way through lighthearted tourists
until they came to the cathedral. Here they turned
right, walking in front of the huge building, before
turning left and passing along its length.

"The cathedral wall was part of the ancient Visigoth
fortifications," David pointed out as they moved under
the huge stone arches.

"Imagine it lasting all these centuries!" Penny
marveled.

They passed the cathedral and found themselves approaching the open-air theater. Here too the streets were crowded. Penny began to feel uneasy.

"Maybe we should start back," she suggested.

"Fine with me," Mark said. David agreed, and the three turned and began to retrace their steps. It was very dark in the narrow stone passageway.

"Let's keep to the right, by the walls," David said. "Then we can cut through to the center of town."

"Mark!" Penny said suddenly as she grabbed her brother's arm. "There's that man again!"

The three stopped suddenly and looked where Penny indicated. But the man had ducked into a doorway and they couldn't see him.

"I know he was there," she said.

"Don't let him know we suspect anything," David said quickly. "Let's just keep on as if we didn't see him."

So that's what they did. They continued walking toward the cathedral, going back the way they'd come.

"Good for you, Penny," Mark said.

"What in the world is he following us for?" she asked anxiously. "Won't those people ever leave us alone?"

"Mark, let's assume he's got a pal," David observed. "Why not lead him on a wild goose chase and lose him in the fortifications?"

"I like that!" Mark replied. "Are you game, Penny?"

"As long as I'm with you guys, I am," she answered.

They wound a tortuous path through the ancient city and its historic walls and turrets. They turned one way, then another; for a while they stood looking at the tall stone walls lit by artificial light. Moving again, the teenagers turned left for a block, then right, following no apparent plan.

But always they were headed back in the direction of the gate through which they'd come. Finally, watching carefully as they moved, they rejoined Jim and Carolyn Daring.

"Let's go," Jim Daring said. "It's getting late." They all walked back to the rental car, got in, and headed back toward their hotel. As soon as they got in the car, the three told their parents about the man who had been following them.

"That settles it!" Jim Daring said. "Enough of this hide-and-seek with these guys. We're going to take our vacation on the coast. Henri told me he wanted us to stay in his house near the beach to the east of Narbonne. We'll drive there tomorrow."

They left the next morning after breakfast, driving the rented car, happy with the prospect of spending several days in their friend's cottage not far from the Mediterranean Sea. The clear blue sky overhead framed the fascinating countryside with its ancient homes, rocky formations, and historic landmarks. Soon they all relaxed and enjoyed the pleasant drive. Danger seemed far away now.

Back in Carcassone, Sergei lifted the receiver and dialed a number in Paris.

Far to the north, in a dingy room in the heart of Paris, the phone rang—once, twice, three times. Grunting with the effort, the heavy man rolled over in his bed and struggled to a sitting position.

The phone rang again: once, twice, three times. Schmidt reached toward the instrument with his powerful arm. When it rang again he lifted the receiver.

"Oui," he said.

"Sergei here," the voice on the other end replied. "Did you get the letter?"

"Yes, we did. Yesterday. But it had been opened. What do you know about that?" Schmidt asked.

"Nothing. It was open when we got it," Sergei said quickly. "We stole it from the hotel room."

"Good work, Sergei!" the man answered. But there was a hesitation in his voice; Sergei became nervous.

"We must know if the Americans opened that letter and copied it," the heavy man said. "Those names include some real weaklings. They're fine when things go well. They write, and they teach, and they'll broadcast for television news programs what we tell them to. But several of those people will crack under any kind of pressure if the police get to them, and then they'll endanger all the others. That's why we've got to know if that list was copied by anyone who would get it to the police."

Sergei sighed. Would this job never end? "What do you want me to do?"

"Just what I said—find out if the Darings copied

that list and sent it to the police."

"How do you suggest I do that?" Sergei asked.

"Get one of those kids, make him talk, and tell me if the answer is yes or no," Schmidt replied. Sergei could tell from his tone that the man's patience was wearing thin. Schmidt spoke again.

"Do whatever is necessary, but make one of those kids talk. We've *got* to know."

"Yes, sir," Sergei replied. But the line was already dead.

Sergei sighed. How would he do what Schmidt wanted? The Americans were never alone; the husband was always with his wife, the two boys always with the girl. How were they going to catch one of them apart to get that information?

CHAPTER 9

THE SECRET PATH

"How can the sea be so blue?" Penny asked, as she strolled with David and Mark along the cliff above the brilliant Mediterranean Sea.

They'd arrived the day before and moved into the quaint small stone home owned by their parents' friend Henri Mevel. Near the ancient port of Narbonne, the white house with red roof was set in a small green valley not far from the sea. Mr. and Mrs. Daring were touring the area in their rented car while the three youngsters explored the rocky shore.

The narrow beach that they were seeking was guarded on each side by tall rock formations, rising like pinnacles from the ground, as if to protect it from any approach. To reach the shore, the three had been told to walk down a winding trail from the cliff above. They moved slowly and carefully in single file, holding sometimes to the thick branches of low bushes that lined the narrow path.

David led, Penny followed, and Mark came last. Even though it was summer, a breeze from the sea made the temperature rather cool on the high ground by which they'd approached the path to the beach.

The path had been cut in the soft stone, probably centuries before, and the footing was very uneven. At first they could see the tall rock cliffs to either side of the beach they sought. But as they descended the narrow winding path, they could no longer see the towers of stone.

"This is like walking in a tunnel" Penny said, as they climbed carefully down the steep passageway.

After a while they came to a wide level spot hemmed in by high stone walls, almost like a room without a ceiling. Here the ground beneath their feet was packed hard. To their right was a thick growth of underbrush in what appeared to be a gap between the huge rocks. They stopped and marveled at the stone walls surrounding them.

"Look!" Penny said, pointing to a series of strange notches in one side of the high rock. These appeared to be climbing upward toward the top. "Those look almost like they were cut into the walls."

"They sure do," Mark replied. "And they're spaced just right for climbing. What's at the top, I wonder?"

"A lookout spot probably, "David suggested. "That side faces the sea, I think, and they could probably see boats from there. I bet smugglers used this place!"

"Maybe they still do!" Mark said, excitement in his voice. "I could climb up there easily!"

"Don't you two try climbing!" Penny warned. "I promised Mom I wouldn't let you do anything foolish, and I've got to keep my promise." They saw she was serious. She didn't like the look of those steps going high up the rock wall.

"Aw, Penny," her brother answered. "That's an easy climb. *You* could make that one."

"Maybe I could, but I won't," she said firmly, "and neither will you."

"Boss, boss, boss, that's all they do to us, David," Mark said resignedly. "And with my binoculars I'd have a great view from the top of that wall."

"You'll have a great view from the beach," Penny answered, "and you won't have to break your neck to see it! There's no need to risk a bad fall to climb up there, and both you boys know it!"

"Let's go, Mark," David said. "When we get her to the beach, we can sneak back and make that climb."

"You will not!" Penny tossed her head and the three turned to resume their downward trek.

Suddenly David stopped and pointed to the thick brush along the stone wall to their right. "Hey! That's almost an opening!" He walked over to the thick bushes packed against the tall stone formation, stooped down, and peered within. "That may be a tunnel!" he said excitedly.

Mark and Penny crowded beside him.

"You're right!" Mark agreed. "We could almost crawl in there!"

"Where do you think it leads? " Penny asked.

"It's heading toward the beach, I think," David replied.

"Watch out for snakes!" Mark said suddenly. He remembered that desperate moment in Pharaoh's tomb, just two weeks ago, when a snake had struck at him and hit his flashlight instead. He still got chills thinking about it.

Penny jumped back with a cry.

Mark laughed, "Well, you can't be too careful, can you?"

"Mark, you're mean!" she cried, realizing that he hadn't actually seen any reptiles.

"Who would have made that tunnel, I wonder?" David asked. He was intrigued by this path that seemed to connect the watch tower with the beach.

Now all of them had a feeling that other people had been present here, people long ago perhaps, people bent on business they didn't want others to know about. Pirates? Smugglers?

They continued their slow descent down the narrow trail between the rock, moving more cautiously now. Each of them had a sense that they were entering into danger. The grey stone walls rose high above them, closing them in—almost like a trap.

"How do we know this leads to the beach?" Penny asked, worried now. "It could be a dead end."

"Henri told Dad about it," Mark replied, "and said it comes out at the shore. There's another path at the eastern end of the beach. But this one is the nearest to our cottage."

"Your dad also said that the path might be overgrown in spots. Henri hadn't been down it for a long time," David reminded them.

"I wouldn't want anyone chasing us down this path," Penny said, "especially since we don't know if we can get out."

"No one's going to chase us," Mark replied, "and we *do* know we can get out. Why are girls so fearful all the time?"

"We're just cautious, that's all," she answered. "After all, we've been chased a lot these last three weeks, ever since David came to visit, in fact."

"Now don't go blaming me again!" he responded. "You people have gotten me in more trouble than I've seen in my whole life!"

Just then their narrow path, so narrow that it almost touched their shoulders on either side, turned to the left—and stopped! A thick wall of bush completely blocked their way.

"How do we get through this?" David asked, standing before the dense green barrier.

Penny peered around his right shoulder, Mark looked around from the left, and they all wondered how they'd get through.

"Well, there's got to be a way," David said, answering his own question, as he reached into the branches and began to pull and shove.

"Hey, it's not too thick!" he exclaimed. "We can move the stuff to the side and make a path. It's not hard to move!"

He pulled branches to one side, moved his body in sideways, and shoved other branches out of his way. Penny squeezed in behind him, and Mark did the same. As they continued forcing their way through the bushes, the light from the outside faded. They were in near-darkness, and barely able to make out what was ahead.

David continued to lead, shoving the green branches to either side, making a path for himself and the others. They followed him, slowly pressing through the tunnel he'd made. The brush and branches moved back into place as they passed through, actually concealing their passing.

The day was pleasantly cool, but this slow pushing through the brush made them all sweat. Step by step they moved through the barricade. The darkness was ominous, Penny thought. What could be ahead?

"Watch out for snakes, David!" she warned.

"There aren't any in this part of the country," he replied.

"Be careful, anyway!" she insisted.

"Look at the light ahead!" David exclaimed suddenly. "We're almost through!"

He came to the final wall of bushes, and began to move these aside. Suddenly he stopped, and Penny bumped into him.

"Don't move!" David whispered. "I see men on the beach!"

CHAPTER 10

SMUGGLERS!

Two men, waist-deep in water, oxygen tanks on their backs, masks on their faces, struggled awkwardly in their flippers toward the shore. Each man carried a rectangular grey box in his arms. A dozen similar boxes were already arranged neatly on the sand, and as the men came out of the water they brought the boxes they carried to this same area and put them down with the others. Then they turned and headed back to sea, stepping high in a strange gait because of the long rubber fins on their feet.

"Look at that!" David whispered, moving aside in the bushes to make room for Penny and Mark. Parting the bushes carefully and squinting in the bright sunlight, the three looked out onto the strange scene. They watched the two divers move out from the shore and then go under water.

"What's going on?" Mark whispered.

"Those men are bringing metal boxes from the water and laying them with the others on the sand," David replied quietly. "I don't see anyone else, but that doesn't mean there's no one around."

"I wonder what's in those boxes?" Penny whispered.

"No telling," David answered. He'd been wondering the same thing.

Just then another man moved into sight from their left, a huge man in dark trousers and dark shirt. Tossing a cigarette to the sand, he approached the line of boxes. The three kids were absolutely still as they watched him pick up one of the grey containers, turn, and walk back out of their vision.

"You were right, David," Mark observed quietly. "Those two in the water aren't the only ones here."

"There could be more, couldn't there?" Penny asked.

"There sure could!" David answered.

"Does this mean we can't go on the beach?" Penny asked.

"I don't think so," Mark said slowly. "But let's wait a few minutes and see if there's anyone else around. This is a hidden beach, Henri told Dad, and those guys might not expect any company."

"Do you think that they're dangerous?" Penny asked.

"I don't know," David said. "But Mark's right. We should watch a while before we go out."

Out of their sight now, the huge man walked up the steep, twisting path in the rocks on the other side of the beach from where Mark, Penny, and David were watching. He sweated as he climbed, cursing audibly at the job they'd given him. *Why won't those guys trade places with me for a half hour*, he wondered, *and let me get in the water and cool off?*

Under the surface of the smooth water between the huge formations of rock that guarded the narrow beach, the two divers would gladly have traded places with the men on shore. The plane had been damaged when it had landed. Only the pilot's skill had brought it safely to a sliding stop before it began to sink. At least it hadn't hit the waves and catapulted! But the right wing had crumpled when the plane sank, and the door on that side had been crushed.

The door on the other side could still be opened, and through this the pilots had escaped and gotten to the surface. However, the plane's fuselage had bent badly when it hit the rocky bottom. The divers could enter the cabin, but had a terrible time getting the valuable containers out of the compartment in the back of the craft.

And it was dangerous for them to try. Just fifteen feet below the surface of the smooth sea, the crushed fuselage was a potential death trap. They'd worked out a method, however. One diver entered the cabin door, then snaked his way carefully toward the back of the craft.

The other diver followed him. The first man squirmed into the fuselage while his companion crouched on the floor and pushed upward against the crumpled ceiling of the cabin to keep a passage open. Inside, twisting in the coffin-like space, the first diver grabbed one of the containers, shoved it toward his helper, and reached for another. One false move and he'd rip off his tank!

With another two boxes recovered, the divers

struggled back through the damaged cabin, squeezed out the narrow door, swam gratefully to the surface and made their way to the beach. When they stood, they began again to walk awkwardly in their flippers to the line of boxes. As before, they deposited the ones they carried and headed back to the water.

"What do you think, Mark?" David asked. "Should we go out on the beach?"

"I don't see why not. They're just divers."

"But how did all those boxes get under the water?" Penny asked. She had a funny feeling about this whole thing, but didn't know how to express it. She wondered if she were being nervous over nothing.

The boys were silent. They had no reason to fear danger in this quiet part of the southern coast of France. After all, the cabin of their friend, Henri, was just a mile away. Would he have loaned it to their family for a week if there were danger nearby?

David had a sudden thought. "We can go left through this brush and come out at another place. That way, we won't reveal the location of this path. We can always retreat by this route if we have to."

"Good idea," Mark observed. "Let's go."

Carefully David began to open a path in the brush to his left, parallel to the beach. Penny and Mark followed him. They labored to make this new path, noticing again how the branches seemed almost to close behind them as they worked their way just along the edge of the sandy beach.

They'd gone about twenty yards when Mark pointed to his left. "Look! There's an opening in the rocks! That may be another path from the cliff to the shore. We can pretend we came from there if they ask any questions."

"Good idea!" David said. "Let's go out on the beach."

But just as they emerged from the brush and stepped out on the beach, the two divers surfaced and began their laborious trek to the shore, each carrying a rectangular grey box in his arms.

Without warning, a gleaming white helicopter swept around the high rock formation to the east of the narrow beach and roared inland to a point just over the heads of the men in the water. It turned suddenly back with deafening noise, then pulled up in a steep climb, and disappeared from sight behind the high rock cliff.

The two divers froze and stared toward the sky.

The big man who'd just left the path and stepped out on the sand froze too.

So did the kids!

The helicopter had seen them all.

"Those divers act scared!" David said. He sensed danger, and so did Mark and Penny. They each wished that they had stayed in the underbrush and not come out in the open—but it was too late to turn back. They were already visible to the men in the water.

"Then we'd better just act natural and keep going," Mark replied.

The three headed for the other path at the far end of the beach—the path from which that big man had just appeared! The path he was now blocking!

"We'd better not show much interest in what they're doing," Penny said, troubled.

"Let's just walk across the sand to the rocks and look for that other path," Mark suggested. "We'd better get away from here!"

"That big man's standing right where we've got to go!" David said.

"Keep walking," Mark replied, "we've got to act natural." They were all scared now.

Mark and David waved to the men emerging from the water as they kept walking along the sand toward the other end of the beach. Would those men in the water chase them? Would the man at the end of the beach let them go by?

David stopped suddenly, lifted the binoculars from the case on his belt, and looked upward at a soaring bird. He pointed, as if that's what the three were looking for. "Don't forget our excuse for being here!" he said quietly. Mark and Penny looked up also.

The huge man still stood at the entrance to the other path, blocking their escape!

The divers had put down their boxes somewhere in the water, and were hurrying to the shore towards them, heading to intercept the three Americans. Instinctively, the kids knew they had to show that they were no threat to these divers!

"We'd better stop and wait to speak to them," Mark whispered.

Penny and David stopped with him.

"Bonjour!" Mark called as the divers left the water, slipped off their flippers, and walked rapidly across the sand towards them.

Both men were stocky and powerfully built. As they approached, the larger of the two, forced a smile. "Bonjour," he replied. Then, speaking rapid French, he asked Mark if they were looking for something.

"Oui," Mark answered, also speaking French. He pointed to the lone bird circling the beach, and told them they were bird-watchers. Their father's business partner, who lived nearby, had sent them to this beach to see the different birds of this region.

The two divers were silent, pondering this. Then the larger one smiled a forced smile again and told Mark they'd find interesting seabirds along the whole southern coast of France. He looked sideways at the other diver.

"Let's rest a while," he said, as he slipped off his tank and let it fall to the sand.

David knew no French at all. Penny had been quietly translating for him all the while, smiling as she did so, appearing to have not a care in the world. *Gosh, she's smart!* David thought to himself.

But Penny had a sinking feeling in her stomach. Were these men going to trap them on the beach?

David stood quietly by as the man spoke rapidly to Mark. But his eyes searched the row of boxes on the sand. There was other gear stashed there too. Then he noticed two automatic rifles lying on a tarp beside the boxes! Quickly he looked away. He couldn't let them know that he'd seen those guns!

Mark grinned at the divers and pointed to David, telling them that their American friend didn't understand French. The larger man began to tell Mark what he and his friend were doing in the water.

Mark translated for David. "He says they're marine biologists. Their motorboat sank just offshore with a lot of the samples they'd collected and they're diving for them. They'll be through in a couple of hours, and we can have the beach to ourselves."

The three Americans breathed a sigh of relief at that! The men were going to let them go!

Mark waved good-bye to the divers and turned. "Let's go," he said. David and Penny started walking with him toward the path where the huge man still stood, arms folded across his chest.

"Drop behind us, Penny," Mark said. "Keep looking up at the rocks for birds."

David and Mark walked ahead of Penny as they moved closer to the man who blocked the path to the cliff above. He was very large and powerfully muscled, with long arms and huge hands. A wide black moustache gave a sinister appearance to his brutal face. Around his powerful neck was tied a thin red bandanna. Dark-skinned from a life in the sun, he loomed larger and larger as the three approached.

He looks cruel, Penny thought to herself as they

came closer. Mark and David had stepped apart a couple of yards as they approached the man—they were ready for anything.

Was he going to let them pass?

CHAPTER 11

THE GATHERING STORM

Inside the noisy cabin of the speeding white helicopter, the pilot spoke bitterly to his companion. "Those fools in Africa bungled! That plane almost got to shore! Did you see it under the water!"

"What happened?" the copilot replied. "They were supposed to fix the engines so they'd stop over the sea!"

"They failed."

"They're diving to get the drugs," the pilot continued. "Did you see those boxes they'd stacked on the beach?"

"I did. We've got to call headquarters right away!"

The pilot had a sudden thought: "Maybe we could swipe those drugs when we wipe out that gang on the beach!"

His companion grinned at the thought. "We could! We'd be killing two birds with one stone; knocking out those guys for muscling into our territory, and getting a fortune from the drugs they brought! They'd be paying for their own funeral—and a lot more, beside!"

The pilot agreed. "Contact Headquarters! Tell them

we don't have time to plan anything elaborate! Now that those men have been spotted, they'll move fast! If we want to get rid of them, and get their stuff, we'll have to move faster than we've ever moved before!"

"I'll call right away!"

The copilot rose from his seat in the speeding craft and moved back to the communications desk. There he activated the coding instruments and prepared his message. The pilot meanwhile kept the helicopter swooping westward along the coast. He didn't dare turn back because that would definitely alert the men in the water. It was just possible that they didn't fear any danger yet. After all, lots of private people and corporations had helicopters. Maybe they hadn't worried about the helicopter's sudden appearance.

But the men on the beach were not fools. As soon as the white helicopter had swooped away, Charles, the leader, grabbed his tank and mask and slipped into his flippers. His companion did the same.

He waved urgently to the big man who'd finally stepped aside to let the three Americans pass. "Call Pierre! Tell him to alert the office in Paris. We've got to get this cargo out of the water and into the van. We may need more men to get out of here!"

The big man ran to the pile of boxes, grabbed one, then hurried across the rocky beach, heading back toward the path that led to the cliff above.

Charles called again as he struggled across the sandy beach. "Tell Pierre to finish that call in a hurry and help you carry these things to the truck. We've got to get out of here before that helicopter returns or calls for help!"

The divers turned and high-stepped laboriously across the sand toward the water, awkwardly lifting their long flippers as they did so. Soon they were in the water, swimming away from the beach. Then they were under, moving swiftly down to the plane on the bottom.

While Charles had been calling out these frantic orders, the three youngsters had walked gratefully past the big man in black and had entered the narrow path that led to the cliff above. Turning around a tall rock wall, they could still hear the diver's shouted instructions to the man they'd just passed.

Mark and Penny knew at once that he would soon be hurrying up the path behind them!

Looking wildly around, Mark noticed a gap in the big stones that flanked the entrance to their left, a gap covered with the same kind of bush they'd tunneled through on the other side of the beach.

"We've got to get out of their way!" he said. "Quick, David! Push another tunnel into that underbrush!"

"We could beat him up the hill," David replied, "because he'll be carrying that box."

"But we'd have to go through the same explanations with their friends at the top. They might not let us go!" Mark said.

"You're right," David agreed.

He turned instantly to his left and began to shove a

way into the leaves and branches between the tall walls of rock. Madly he forced himself through the underbrush, while Penny and Mark followed as fast as they could. Just inside the thick green mass, Mark turned and bent back the branches so as to cover the entrance. Then he whispered to Penny, "Tell David to stop a minute. We've got to let that man pass and we don't want him to hear us breaking through this brush!"

Penny grabbed David's shoulder and whispered the message in his ear. She held his arm as the three of them knelt, absolutely still in the stifling closeness of the brush.

Had they gone far enough from the path? Would the big man see the branches they'd moved? Would he call the others to capture them? If he did, there was no way they could escape.

With hearts pounding in the darkness of their hiding place, Mark, Penny, and David waited for the man to pass. Unconsciously they held their breath.

Then they heard his feet crunching along the stones of the beach, directly toward them! Breathing audibly with the burden he carried, the man approached their hiding place—and kept going! He climbed upward, moving on the steep winding passageway with difficulty because of the heavy load.

The teenagers breathed again!

"We've got to run back across the beach while those men are still in the water!" David said.

Mark led as the three pushed their way out of the

dense underbrush and peered around the rocks toward the beach.

The divers were not visible!

"They've gone under water!" David said gratefully. "We can make it back to our tunnel! Let's go!"

The three raced across the rocky beach toward the spot from which they'd first come out of the brush.

"I hope we can find it!" David said as they ran, searching frantically for the place.

"There it is!" Penny cried, recognizing the spot. This was not the first time—nor would it be the last—that the boys were grateful that she'd trained herself to observe and then remember what she'd seen!

They ran to the place she pointed out and halted. David began forcing a way through the thick underbrush. Penny and Mark followed. Once inside the dense stuff, Mark turned and bent back the branches to cover the spot they'd entered.

Now they were once again struggling through thick branches and leaves. It was slow going. And it was hot.

How long would it take them to get back to the path which had brought them from the cliff to the beach?

Meanwhile, on the high ground above the beach, two hundred yards to the west of the tall rocks toward which the three were climbing, a dark blue Mercedes pulled off the narrow road, bumped across the rough ground, and parked behind a pile of rocks. Four men got out.

The usually elegantly suited Sergei now wore faded

jeans and a black sweater. His companions wore the same. Almost a uniform for so many Europeans, the clothes were suited for rough work—which was exactly what these men were planning! Sergei leaned against the car and unfolded a map.

"Here we are," he pointed. "We'll take that path to the beach.

"How do we know the kids are still there?" Uri asked. He was in a better mood now that they were going into action! No more of this waiting game! He grinned at the thought of cornering those kids.

"We tapped their phone," Sergei replied. "We heard the mother call a friend in Paris and say that the kids planned to spend several hours on the beach today. The girl's a photographer, and they're going to look for birds."

"What's the plan?" Marcel asked. Short, stocky, he looked the most vicious of the four. Scars from past fights marred his brutal thick face. Powerful arms and legs bulged in the rough clothes he wore, and a dirty black beret topped an otherwise bald head.

"We'll sneak up on them from two directions at once," Sergei said. "Two of us go down to the beach by the path on this side, two go down the other side. They'll be trapped between us! When we spot them, we'll just move out and cover them with our guns. I'll ask about the letter. If they hesitate, Marcel will grab the girl and make her talk. It's as simple as that. We've *got* to know if they made copies of that letter and sent them to anyone else! And time's running out! If the police have that list, they'll be arresting some of our people soon—we've *got* to know so we can warn as many as we can!"

"I'll make her talk," Marcel said quietly.

"The beach has two paths," Sergei continued, "one at the west end and one on the east. Right now, we're approaching the western path. When we get to the top of the cliff, Uri and Jacques will keep going and head for the eastern path. Marcel and I will go down the near one, but not until you two are ready to go down too. The kids should be on the beach. Uri and I have radios; he'll signal when he and Jacques have reached the far path and are ready to start down. At the bottom, we'll talk again. We want to move out onto the beach at the same time. Those kids are trapped. They won't have a chance! Any questions?"

There were none. "Let's go," Sergei said with a triumphant smile.

Marcel grinned a wicked grin. He'd make that girl talk!

CHAPTER 12

"TIME'S RUNNING OUT!"

Desperately the two divers struggled into the narrow confines of the sunken plane. Taking turns at the most dangerous part of the task, they removed two more of the boxes and brought these to the shore.

They stood, dripping water, resting for a minute above the row of boxes, breathing heavily, and beginning to feel the strain of the job.

"This is taking too much time," Charles said. "Let's stay down longer and bring all the boxes out of the plane. We'll just stack them on the ocean floor, and go back inside until we've got them all out. Then we can bring them to the shore and be done with it!"

The other man agreed and they returned to the dangerous underwater trap. Charles stayed inside the crushed part of the fuselage, shoving out one box after another. His companion picked these up one by one and backed out of the compartment and the opened door. Outside the plane, he laid the boxes on the rocky bottom and went back into the cabin.

After several trips, he snaked his way back into the fuselage, grabbed Charles's arm, pointed to himself, and indicated he'd trade places.

Charles nodded, then turned slowly, and came out of the cramped area. His muscles screamed with the agony of staying bent in that confined coffin, and he welcomed the chance to stack the boxes while his companion took his place in the narrow confines of the fuselage.

But everything took so long! They moved as if in slow motion in the murky water inside the plane, and both men couldn't help wondering what was going on above the surface of the sea. Had the helicopter returned? Had it radioed for help? And was it merely a private craft. Or had their enemies found them?

Charles had a sudden thought. He'd just carried another box from the plane and laid it on the sea floor, when the idea struck him. They should quit now! They should get away with what they'd already retrieved. It would bring a fortune on the black market and they shouldn't risk life imprisonment or death for a few more boxes.

This decided, Charles acted at once. Moving carefully into the cabin of the sunken plane, he pulled himself back to the crushed fuselage. There were two more of the boxes that his companion had stacked. Charles grabbed the man's arm.

Startled, the man looked back over his shoulder. With his other hand Charles jerked his thumb in the universal sign which meant "Get out!" The man nodded, relieved.

Picking up one of the boxes, Charles struggled backward out of the plane. His companion did the same. They emerged, swam to the surface, and kicked rapidly toward shore.

Once on the beach, they pushed back their SCUBA masks and deposited the boxes. "Let's get out with what we've got!" Charles said. "I've got a funny feeling about that helicopter!"

Just then the big man in black ran down the path and onto the beach, with Pierre right behind him.

"We've got help coming," Pierre yelled to the divers. "By boat. They'll back us up with four more men!"

"When will they get here?"

"Fifteen minutes," Pierre replied.

"Then get this stuff up to the van," Charles said. "We'll go back for two more boxes on the bottom. That's all. The fish can have the rest."

Vastly relieved by the leader's decision to get out so quickly, the men set to work with a will. Only fools didn't know when to quit!

Meanwhile, twenty miles to the east and five miles inland from the sea, the gleaming white helicopter had landed in a farmyard. Two men rushed from a parked car, carrying assault rifles and ammunition, and crowded into the waiting craft whose rotors had slowed but not stopped. Once the men were inside, the pilot revved the engines. The helicopter lifted gracefully, swooped to the left in a tight turn, and headed back toward the hidden beach, flying low over the water.

Inside the cabin of the speeding craft, one of the men in jungle fatigues crowded toward the front, leaned between the pilot and copilot, and spoke over the terrible racket from the engines. "The boss is very pleased that you found those scum! Now we'll have our revenge!"

The pilot smiled with satisfaction. "What about reinforcements? Will we have more men?"

"We will," the man replied, bright teeth gleaming in his dark face. "They're coming in the speedboat. They'll hit that beach in just twenty minutes, and he wants us to do the same. We can hang off the beach a few kilometers until we see the boat coming below us, and then time our arrival to match theirs. We'll wipe out those scum on the beach before they know what's happening. Then you'll lift us to the top of the cliff and we'll get that van before it can move. We'll take all the boxes of drugs in it, and the crew on the boat will collect what they find on the beach. There's a fortune there!"

"What a plan!" the copilot said admiringly. "They'll be hit from the air and the sea at the same time! The divers won't be able to fight even if they happen to be on shore. They're in diving gear, and they sure can't run for their guns wearing those flippers!"

"Speaking of guns," the copilot added, "let me go and collect mine. Too bad you're going to miss this," he grinned at the pilot. "That's what comes from being a taxi driver!" He got up and moved back toward the storage area. One of the men they'd just picked up took his seat beside the pilot.

"Whatever made those fools think they could muscle into our North African territory?" the pilot asked him. "Don't they know what we did to the last group that tried that? We got them all!"

"They're just dumb," the man in jungle fatigues replied, "just dumb."

Miles to the east of the speeding helicopter, Sergei's men approached the cliff above the beach. They had hurried through the tall swaying grass amid weather-beaten trees and bald rocks. Now they were close to the path that led downward to the sea.

"Time to separate!" Sergei commanded.

Marcel and Uri turned left and headed rapidly toward the high rock formation guarding the eastern side of the hidden beach below. Sergei waited a few minutes, smoking, giving those two time to reach the top of the path.

At the eastern edge of the cliff, ahead of Marcel and Uri, but hidden from their view behind the hilly ground, Pierre and the big man had just returned to the van with more of the boxes of drugs they'd brought up from the beach.

"I hate leaving the van unguarded like this," Pierre grumbled. A short plump man, in jeans and red shirt, his pale face contrasted with the dark complexion of his huge companion. Both men wore guns now, automatics stuck in their belts. Pierre also carried an automatic rifle slung over his shoulder.

"Who's going to bother the van?" the big man asked contemptuously. This little squirt was the most fearful man he'd worked with this year, always worrying about something that never happened!

He continued to try to calm the frightened little fellow. "The van's hidden in these trees. No one can see it from the trail we came in on, and no one can see through these branches from the air. Who's going to bother it?"

"I know, I know," the little man said irritably. "But we make it a rule never to leave our vehicles without a guard.

"I don't like leaving our only way out of here without someone to watch it!" They put the boxes in the van and headed back toward the path that led down to the beach.

"Well, we have to do it!" the big man continued as they went. "Orders are orders. And, frankly, they make sense. We don't know who was in that helicopter—it could be the police, it could be another gang trying to steal our drugs, it could be anybody. It makes sense to get out while we can. Charles is smart. He's been doing this for years. And when he smells trouble, I say we should do what he tells us to!"

Pierre wasn't even listening. "There's another thing," he complained, puffing as he struggled to keep up with the big man on the narrow, steep, and very uneven path down to the beach. "We're leaving a lot of boxes in that plane, maybe a third of them! That's a ton of money we could be throwing away!"

"We can't spend it if we're dead or in jail," the big man answered.

They were hurrying down the steep path now, the big man leading and Pierre following with great difficulty. They didn't see Uri and Jacques sneak up to the grove of trees at the top of the path above and behind them.

Uri took out his radio and called Sergei. "We're at the top of the path," he said softly.

Just over a hundred yards away, hidden behind the hill, Sergei was holding his radio in hand, waiting for the message.

"Excellent," he replied. "Let's go!"

With drawn pistols the four KGB agents began their slow descent, two from the west, two from the east. "Those teenagers on the beach are trapped!" Sergei whispered to his companion. The man grinned back.

Unknown to the KGB men, a helicopter and a motorboat, each with armed men aboard, were racing toward the beach from the west.

From the opposite direction, another motorboat with armed men was also racing toward the beach to reinforce Charles and his men on the shore.

CHAPTER 13

THE TRAP IS SPRUNG!

"Be careful, David!" Penny said anxiously. He was leading them rapidly up the steep path that had been cut long ago through the sandstone cliff, hurrying to get away from the men on the beach.

"Don't worry," David replied. He was taking long steps, sometimes pulling himself on the brush that grew between the rocks on either side.

Mark came last, glancing back repeatedly to see if they were being followed. "Those men were still underwater when we got here," he said. "They won't know we're going back this way."

"We'll be at the top before that big man in black comes down," David replied. "By the time they can get together and compare notes, we'll be a long way from here!"

"The helicopter really worried them, didn't it?" Penny asked.

"It sure did!" Mark answered.

"I wonder what's in those boxes." Penny looked

from one to the other. "That's got to be the key to what's going on down on the beach!"

"Whatever it is, those guys are in a hurry to get it out of the water!" Mark chipped in. "And they're really afraid of the helicopter. That's why they told the big man to have the truck driver speed things up. They want to get away as fast as they can!"

"Was that a police helicopter?" she asked.

"It didn't have police markings," David replied. "It looked like a civilian job to me."

"Then why would the divers have been afraid of it?" she asked. Something about the setup worried her.

"I don't know," David answered. "But they're afraid of someone. Did you see those machine guns on the beach?"

Both Mark and Penny nodded. Wisely, none of the three had given the divers any indication that they'd seen the weapons lying by the boxes on the ground.

They were scrambling rapidly up the winding passageway, laboring now. The three of them were all in excellent shape, but the going was tough.

Penny stumbled and almost fell. Mark grabbed her by the waist and steadied her. "Can we rest a minute?" she asked.

"We sure can," Mark said, stopping at once. "Let's save our energy. After all, we've got a long head start."

"And those guys have other things to worry about beside us!" David added. "We're safe."

They leaned against the stone walls, which towered

above them on either side, and caught their breath. Then Mark had an idea.

"Remember that stone wall with the steps cut into it? If we could climb those, we could see what's going on down below."

"Say, you're right!" David said. "I'll go up when we get there and see what I can see."

"I thought of it first!" Mark insisted. "I'll go up!"

This time, Penny didn't object. She knew they should try to find out all they could, and a view from the watchtower might help.

"I'm rested now," she said.

Her brother hugged her reassuringly. She hugged him back and smiled at David. He turned and led them again up the steep path.

Soon they came to the wide room-like space, surrounded on all sides by tall walls of rock. Again they saw the strange tunnel in the brush between the rock formations, and here also were the cuts in the rock that looked as if they'd been made for climbing.

"Be careful, Mark," Penny said anxiously, as her brother walked toward the lower indentations in the wall.

"You can count on that," he said with a grin at his sister. He put his hand in the holes above his head, and began to climb slowly up the sheer wall, placing his feet in the holes his hands had gripped. "This is easy!" he said, moving upward swiftly.

Penny grabbed David's arm as her brother went higher and higher. Near the top, Mark turned his head and looked back the way they'd come.

"I can see part of the path below," he said. "Most of it's hidden, but I can see patches." Then he climbed over the top and disappeared from their view.

Mark climbed down into a roughly circular six-foot-deep chamber surrounded by rock walls but open at the top. There was a level space in the middle, maybe ten feet across. What looked like a drainage hole had been cut into the wall on the southern side toward the sea. Indentations like those he'd used for his climb dotted all four sides of the chamber so that a lookout here could observe from every direction. Stepping to the south wall, Mark put his hands and feet in the holes and climbed up a foot, just high enough to peer over the wall toward the sea.

Before him stretched the brilliant blue water of the Mediterranean. Below was the strip of sandy beach from which they'd just come. And on the beach Mark saw the figures of hurrying men as they picked up the rectangular metal boxes and carried them across the sand to the far edge of the beach, heading for the path that was out of his sight.

But in the water off the beach he could see the outline of the downed aircraft! "That's where they were getting those boxes," he said to himself.

Jumping down from the steps, he crossed to the side from which he'd come and stepped into the places carved for lookouts. Peering over the edge, he called down to David and Penny in as quiet a tone as he could manage. "There's a plane under the water, just off the beach! That's where they were diving for those boxes! There's no boat there at all!"

Relieved at seeing his wide friendly face again, Penny and David pondered his words.

"They were lying to us then," David said.

"Why?" Penny asked. "Unless they were doing something illegal!"

"I guess we know now what's in those boxes," David said somberly.

"And why those men were afraid of the helicopter," Penny said quickly. "They're afraid someone's coming back after them, aren't they?"

"I bet they are!" Mark said.

A small stone bounced down the path, bounced around the turn in the rock, and hit the level stone area where David and Penny stood.

Instantly they froze. Mark looked quickly up the path from where the stone had fallen—and his heart sank!

"Quick!" he whispered. "Hide! There are men coming!"

Hide? David thought helplessly. *Where could they hide in this narrow passage? And they couldn't go back down toward the beach!* Frantically David looked around, saw the tunnel-like hole in the underbrush that he'd noticed before, grabbed Penny's hand, and pulled her toward it. "Get in quick! I'll follow and close up the hole!" he whispered, shoving her ahead of him.

Desperately she crawled into the narrow opening in

the brush and pushed ahead through the thick bushy branches. David crawled in after her; then he turned and began to arrange the branches to cover the opening, pulling them down from above as well as from each side. He'd just barely finished covering the entrance when he heard steps striking the rocks.

Penny and David froze again. Again they held their breath while dangerous men approached. They were barely inside the wall of brush. Would they be visible to people in the path? Would the men see the hole through which they'd crawled?

If they did, David knew they were trapped! They couldn't crawl fast enough to get away. And they had no idea what was ahead of them in the thick brush.

High in the tower above, Mark stepped down to the floor of the lookout tower so he couldn't be seen by the approaching men. Who in the world were they? They had pistols in their hands! Were they with the gang diving for the boxes in the sunken plane or with the people in the helicopter? What was going on?

His mind whirled with these confused thoughts and questions as he heard the men enter the big clear space below him and come to a halt.

Just a few feet from Penny and David, the two KGB agents halted their quiet approach.

"I thought I heard voices," Sergei said very softly in French.

"Maybe it's those kids coming back," Marcel replied, grinning with anticipation.

"Let's wait a minute and listen."

In the darkness of the thick brush, Penny and David sat side by side, trying not to make a sound. His right arm was around her shoulder, his left hand held both of hers. He squeezed gently. She rested her head on his shoulder and prayed silently. David was praying also.

And so was Mark high in the tower above.

A minute went by. Then another. No one moved. Insects began to make small noises in the brush. A lone bird flew high above them.

Sergei and Marcel waited and listened, pistols ready in their hands.

CHAPTER 14

THE FORCES CONVERGE

The high-speed black boat bounced madly eastward across the bright blue sea, racing along the coast toward the hidden beach. Powerful engines drove the craft over thirty knots an hour, but the ride was awful! The sea was uneven and the boat crossed the sea's small waves at an angle that bounced it badly, shaking up everything inside—including the passengers.

These four men were shaken so badly that two of them had become violently sick all over the floor of the boat.

"Slow down!" the squat man in dungarees and dirty shirt yelled again at the fat man behind the wheel. "Slow down before you kill my men!"

The man at the helm ignored him as hc'd been doing for half an hour.

With a wild flame in his eyes the squat man pulled his 9 millimeter automatic pistol and jammed it deep into the fat man's side.

Grunting with pain, alarmed now, the man pulled back the throttle and the boat slowed slightly. Instantly, the ride improved a hundred per cent!

The two sick men sat weakly on the floorboards and leaned against the side of the boat, assault rifles clutched in their hands across their laps. The men looked awful. Belts with ammunition clips littered the floor, and their canteens were scattered with the other gear. The whole mess had been sliding across the floorboards with every bounce of the boat.

At the slower speed, still in excess of twenty knots, the ride was tolerable. Gradually the sick men began to show signs of life.

"What a mess!" the squat man said to his lieutenant, a powerfully built man, also dressed in jungle fatigues, who slouched against the side of the boat.

The leader spoke again. "We're attacking an armed gang in fifteen minutes, and this fool of a boat jockey makes half our force sick with his wild driving!" Looking somberly at the man at the wheel, he said quietly to his lieutenant, "I think I'll kill him when we wipe out those cutthroats on the beach."

His lieutenant nodded, long dark hair falling into his face as he did so. Why not? The fool had refused to slow the boat until the boss had pulled his pistol and jabbed him with it. Was the guy high on the drugs he stole?

The high curving white wakes swept up and away from the black bow as it cut through the shining blue Mediterranean. The two men leaned their heads together and reviewed the battle plan.

They would attack the beach through the narrow

opening in the rocks just as the helicopter came over the water to join them. It would be a complete surprise! They'd wipe out the men on shore. The helicopter would then attack any men still on the cliff with the van and load the drugs. Then it would return to the beach. After that, they'd race out to sea—and safety!

The plan was simplicity itself. Those smugglers on the beach had no idea of what was coming.

Ahead of the speeding boat, Charles's unsuspecting gang on the beach had not been idle. Pierre and the big man had just rushed another two containers up the terrible path, dumped them in the van, and were rushing down the path again. Unknown to them, they were just ahead of the unsuspecting KGB agents, Uri and Jacques, who were also descending the path, expecting only to find the unarmed American teenagers!

The big man and Pierre hurried down the steep path again, careful not to turn their ankles in the uneven passageway. Their spirits rose at the prospect of a quick end to this dangerous enterprise; soon they'd be far away. And they'd be rich!

Still separated from each other by a few miles, the two speedboats rushed toward the hidden beach. The white one came from the east, with reinforcements for Charles and the divers. The black boat roared in from the west with men from the rival gang that had sabotaged the plane in Africa. They planned to attack Charles's group in coordination with the helicopter still swooping low over the water behind them.

None of the men in either boat knew they were heading for a boatload of armed enemies! Neither gang knew that Sergei and three other KGB agents were converging on the same beach, guns in hand.

Back on the steep stone passageway to the western side of the beach, time stood still. David and Penny were frozen in the dark closeness of the thick underbrush, not daring to move or make a sound.

Finally Sergei spoke quietly to Marcel. "There's no one here. Let's go."

The two men continued their careful descent to the beach. Sergei led the way, stepping softly around the edge of the stone wall, easing down the rough path, gun ready. Marcel followed him down the narrow, curving passage. Slowly they moved out of the hearing of the three teenagers.

But still the three Americans waited. No one moved; no one made a sound that might alert those men and bring them back. Maybe they had just pretended to leave. Maybe they were just around the turn in the rock, waiting for the slightest sound.

Mark dared not look over the top of the watchtower—one of the men might be looking. If they saw him in that tower, he was trapped!

David and Penny heard the soft footfalls of the two men as they began again to descend the path, but they didn't dare move back into the path. Men could be coming from either direction, and then they'd be trapped.

David thought about what to do; then he made up his mind.

"Penny, we can't call Mark. Those men might hear us! And we can't take a chance of getting caught in that narrow pathway. We've got to follow this tunnel and see where it comes out. Then we can run back to the house and call the police!"

"But we can't leave Mark!" she said, anxiety clouding her dark brown eyes.

"He's safe as long as he stays in that tower!" David answered. "But we're his only hope—we've got to get help for him."

She nodded in the thick darkness.

He squeezed her hand, then turned and began to crawl along the narrow tunnel, shoving the branches to the side, forcing a path through the ancient passageway. He wondered how long it had been since anyone had crawled through? Where would it take them?

Penny crawled slowly behind David through the slender passage in the matted underbrush. Thick branches scraped their skin as they moved; sweat soaked their clothes from the heat in the thicket where no breeze could enter.

"This tunnel has been used before," he said quietly over his shoulder.

"Who do you think made it?" she whispered.

"Maybe smugglers," he replied. "We may learn more when we get to the end."

High in the tower behind them, Mark ventured a

quick look toward the beach. The divers had come out of the water for good, it seemed. Their gear was flung on the rocky surface, and they were carrying the gray boxes toward the path at the beach's east end.

Mark looked back up the path where he and David and Penny had originally come down. There was no one in sight in the few spots he could examine. The rocks hid most of the deeply cut passage from his view, however, and there was no way he could be sure it was clear.

Finally he dared to peer over the edge and look directly below—the men with the pistols had gone! He'd heard them move, but hadn't dared look because he suspected an ambush. But they were no longer in sight.

What should I do, he wondered? If he climbed down, he would still be trapped if those men came back up the trail.

On the other hand, they were clearly looking for danger—with their guns in hand—so they must be enemies of the men on the beach.

They'll probably keep going down toward the beach, he thought to himself. *That means the way back up the path should be safe now.*

He realized that Penny and David were not only hidden in that tunnel—they were trapped! And there was no telling how far they'd crawled into that underbrush. He knew he didn't dare call them, for fear of alerting the men with guns. Mark knew he had to try to get out and find help.

Looking all around again, he noticed something else

along the top of the beach. A road was partially visible, a half mile to the west or so. More a dirt path than road, it was nevertheless wide enough for cars. If he could get to that, he might flag a car and get a ride. That would be quicker than retracing the trail they'd taken from the house.

Mark studied the whole area again. Breathing deeply, he clambered up the steps, crawled over the top of the wall, and began the descent to the path. It took a moment for his feet to find the slots in the wall below him. Holding to the steps cut into the rock, he lowered himself slowly, feeling blindly with his feet for each succeeding hole. He thought the climb down would never end. He was a naked target if anyone came along the path!

But soon he was near the bottom. He dropped the last few feet and began to move up the steep passage as quickly as he could. At least Penny and David were safe in the underbrush. He stepped quietly to the edge of the thick growth and tried to see within. He could detect no one there.

Maybe they crawled farther into this brush, he thought.

But if anyone came down the path now, Mark realized that he'd be caught. *I've got to get out of here!*

It was an agonizing climb to the hilltop above, but he met no one. Reaching the top, Mark looked carefully around, then chose a path that took him behind bushes and trees. He began to run in the direction of the road he'd seen from the watchtower. Half expecting a shout—or a shot—behind him, he covered yard after yard in his easy stride.

I'm going to get away with this! he thought exultantly to himself. Now to flag a car and get help for David and Penny.

But would a car stop for a stranger, he wondered suddenly. The people here were not too cordial to strangers, he'd found. He might have to run all the way back to the house if he couldn't stop a vehicle.

Suddenly Mark came upon Sergei's blue Mercedes! Hidden from the road behind a high pile of rock, it was also partially concealed by a clump of bushes. Mark dropped to the ground at once. Was anyone inside the car? Breathing heavily from his run, he crawled behind a thicket. Peering through the branches he studied the car—it was empty! He searched carefully, but saw no one in the area. Slowly he rose and approached the Mercedes.

When he reached the vehicle, he could see how cleverly it had been hidden from the dirt road. No one would have seen it had they driven by. Opening the driver's door, he looked inside. The keys were not there; he hadn't really thought they would be. Quickly he searched the front seats and then looked in the glove compartment.

Here he found a surprise—a packet of three flares and some maps! Standard flares of the kind used by boats and hikers, they seemed to offer possibilities. He found nothing else.

I bet those men with the guns came in this car, he thought to himself as he stood up and looked again around him.

How long would it take for him to find a car that would give him a ride? How long would David and Penny be able to escape being found by those armed men?

Who were the other men who came in the car? And the helicopter? Something violent was brewing and he had to help David and Penny get out of it!

CHAPTER 15

"THEY'LL NEVER KNOW WHAT HIT THEM!"

The white boat with reinforcements for Charles raced around the rocky promontory guarding the eastern edge of the hidden beach and swept through the narrow channel. The men on board held their automatic rifles ready as the craft slowed and approached the beach.

Waving madly, Charles rushed knee-deep into the water and motioned the boat over to the beach. The man behind the wheel reversed the engine, and the boat swung gently to a stop, just fifteen yards from the shore.

"Over there!" Charles called, pointing toward the rocks to his right, "There's a little docking area just behind that tall rock. You can tie up right to the shore."

Waving acknowledgment, the man behind the wheel put the boat in motion again and took it around the large high rock that concealed the boat slip. He came in from the beach side, slowed as he neared the grey stone, and had one of the other men jump out with a line and secure the boat to the rocks. Another man stepped out from the stern and tied onto a rock.

The men jumped out with their automatic rifles, hurried along a rock path until they reached the sandy shore, and then ran to Charles who was waiting for them by the pile of metal boxes.

"Take as many as you can!" Charles called, as he began to collect his diving gear.

There were only ten of the containers left. Soon the men had six of these in the boat, while Charles's other two men picked up the remaining boxes and took them up the path to the van.

"What a haul!" Charles said, exulting, as he gathered his diving gear and stuffed it into a large plastic sack. "We've got almost all the boxes from the plane. The fish can get high on the rest!"

The men laughed.

Very close now, but still out of sight behind the rocks, the helicopter swept low across the calm sea from the west, so low that the rotors swept up a trail of water behind the speeding craft.

"There's our black boat!" the copilot said, pointing down. "We're timing this perfectly. Those scum won't know what hit them!"

The pilot laughed triumphantly. They'd strike that gang unexpectedly, wipe them out, and retrieve the drugs!

Back in Paris, Schmidt was sweating. Not that his

room was hot—it was a cool day. But he'd had no word from Sergei for a long time. What was causing the delay?

Worse, he'd been unable to reach four of the people he'd called, people on that list they'd just retrieved from the American girl's camera case! Where could they be? It wasn't likely that they'd all be gone at the same time. He *had* to alert them that their security might have been compromised.

Again he lifted the phone and dialed the number Sergei had given him. In the last call Sergei had told of his success in following the Americans to the cottage near the shore where the family planned to stay. Wonder of wonders, he'd even been able to sneak to the house at night and attach a listening device to their phone line!

Then, just the day before, he'd called to say that the three kids planned to walk to the beach the next morning. "This is our chance," Sergei had told him. "We'll follow them, grab the girl, and make her tell us if they passed that list to the police! I'll call you as soon as we get back."

But it was afternoon now, and Sergei hadn't called. What had happened on that beach? Had Sergei and his men captured the girl and gotten the information he needed? If they had, why hadn't he called to let him know?

He reached into the cigarette pack; it was empty. Angrily he threw it across the room and thrust his hand into the desk drawer for another pack. How could three American teenagers cause so much trouble to a network of professional spies? He was outraged at the situation, but could do nothing about it. Sergei hadn't called; the people in Paris hadn't answered. What was going on?

That's the question David asked himself as he and Penny crawled through the partially blocked tunnel in the underbrush. Suddenly they heard the sound of a boat's engines; then the sound ceased.

"Who was that?" she asked him anxiously, crawling up close beside him in the narrow way. It was so dark in the brush that they could barely see in the dim light that filtered through the branches.

"I don't know," David replied, utterly confused. "But that boat is close. It sounds like it's just ahead of us. That means we're almost at the shore. I guess this tunnel was made to connect to the watchtower Mark climbed."

"Stay here a minute, Penny," he said suddenly. "I'll look ahead and see what's going on."

"Please be careful, David," she said.

"Don't worry, I will. I'll be right back." He squeezed her hand, then began to crawl quietly through the dark narrow passage.

High above them, back on the level ground behind the steep rock cliffs, Mark ran along the dirt trail that was obviously a path for vehicles. Still carrying the three flares in his hand as he ran, he hoped to spot a car or truck that would take him back to a phone.

But the trail turned suddenly to his right and headed back toward the beach! Alarmed now, Mark slowed his pace. The beach was the last place he wanted to go! Yet the trail *had* to swerve back toward a road! So it offered the fastest way for him to reach help for Penny and David. He had no choice but to continue.

Mark ran for another hundred yards along the path that was partially concealed at this point by trees on either side. Suddenly he stopped—directly to his right, off the trail, an unmarked van was parked!

Hiding behind a clump of bushes, Mark peered anxiously through the leaves. Was there anyone around? If so, Mark knew that he didn't dare let himself be seen! He froze as his eyes searched the area.

But he saw no one.

Mark crept toward the van, concealing himself behind clumps of bushes as he moved. Soon he was close to the vehicle. Again he froze and looked all around. Again he saw no one. Nor did he hear the sounds of anyone moving. He moved swiftly toward the van and looked inside. The keys were in the ignition!

The next minute he was in the driver's seat, turning the key, pressing the accelerator, and starting the engine! The motor roared into life and the van lurched over the uneven ground, turned onto the narrow trail, increased speed and roared away, raising a cloud of dust as it went.

Mark was ecstatic! The terrible helplessness that

had gripped him for so long was gone! Now he could get to a phone, and call the police! He prayed that David and Penny would keep themselves hidden until help arrived.

But just at the edge of the beach, David had crawled to the end of the tunnel in the thick underbrush and looked through the branches that closed it. He could barely make out the outlines of an open boat. Just fitting into a narrow cove between the high rocks on each side, the white craft was pointing out to the sea.

David pushed aside the branches to his left so he could get a view of the beach. There he saw a gang of men clustered on the rocky shore almost sixty yards away. No one was even close to the boat!

Quickly he turned and crawled back through the dark passage to Penny. In the darkness of the tunnel he couldn't see her face break into a huge smile of relief when he returned.

"What did you find?" she whispered.

"A boat!" he replied. "There's a group of men on the beach, around a pile of stuff, but no one's near the boat. I think we can take it and get out of here. We've got to get away and find help for Mark. He'll be stuck in that tower until we do! Let's go while those men are still on the beach."

Quickly the two crawled along the passage in the bush. When they came to the end, which was covered with branches, David stopped. Turning, he whispered to Penny, "Let me look again and make sure they're still out of the way."

He forced his way again through the brush to his left, and found the place from which he'd looked out onto the beach. Would the men still be there? Would they be far enough away for him and Penny to take the boat and get out of that hidden harbor? He had to get her out of this danger!

Fearfully, he parted the brush and peered through.

CHAPTER 16

DRUG WAR

The men were still gathered at the other end of the beach, at least sixty yards away.

Quickly David crawled back to Penny. "They're still a long way down the beach. Let's grab that boat and get out of here!"

He parted the bushes that concealed the tunnel from the hidden boat shelter and the two of them ran toward the rocking craft. The large mass of rock thrusting up from the water ten yards away hid the boat slip from the men on the shore. David rushed toward the bow, lifted the rope tied around a pile of rocks, and tossed it on the deck. Penny did the same to the line at the stern. Then they both jumped into the cockpit.

Searching quickly for the controls, David noticed the two assault rifles lying on the floor, and the clips of ammunition in the belts beside them.

"What's going on?" he asked incredulously.

Hurriedly he sat in the seat behind the wheel of the white boat and reached for the key to the ignition as Penny got into the seat to his left. Between them was a narrow passage to the space under the front deck.

"Here goes!" he said somberly, as he put his hand

on the ignition key. "Keep praying!"

Before he could turn the key, the peaceful beach exploded with sudden violence. The black boat filled with armed men roared into the harbor from the west, a huge white wake curving into the air behind and on each side, and swept to its left. Just at that minute a helicopter soared in from the same direction and swerved to the right. Automatic rifles from the boat and the helicopter sprayed the beach in a shocking attack!

Charles and his completely surprised men threw themselves frantically on the sand. They lifted the automatic rifles they carried and blazed back at the attacking boat and helicopter.

Several men bolted for the trail at the eastern end of the beach, while the men who'd come in the white boat started to dash back for their craft behind the large rock—just where David and Penny were! But these men were turned back and pinned down by automatic fire from the black boat that was racing madly along the shore, spewing streams of bullets.

Kneeling on the beach, Charles and two of his crew returned the deadly fire with carefully controlled bursts from their own automatic rifles. Splinters of wood flew from the bow of the speeding boat, and the windshield shattered under the fire. Inside the cockpit of the bouncing craft, men fired back.

Sergei and Marcel had just crawled out of the tunnel from the rock path and stood on the beach, not far from the white boat. Charles spotted them at once. Mistaking them for members of the attacking team, he opened fire with his automatic rifle, sick with apprehension that he and his fellow smugglers were being attacked from the air, the sea—and from the land behind!

Sergei and Marcel, utterly shocked, threw themselves desperately to the ground and fired back at Charles and his men with their pistols. Expecting to spring a trap on unarmed and unsuspecting American teenagers, they'd been stunned by the sudden gunfire and the sight of armed men with assault rifles firing at them! Instinctively they blazed away in self-defense.

Shocked to be fired at from that area of the beach, two more of the drug runners turned with their automatic rifles and let loose a volley at the KGB agents. Sergei and Marcel scrambled madly to their left and settled behind the rocks at the edge of the beach.

The men who'd come in the white boat to reinforce Charles's party were now unable to move toward their craft while Sergei and Marcel and machine guns in the boat and helicopter were still blazing away at them!

On the other side of the beach, the other two KGB men, Uri and Jacques, had been similarly surprised. For all his laziness and complaining, Pierre was a terror with automatic weapons. His first burst swept the trail before him. Uri and Jacques threw themselves frantically to the ground, shocked and surprised but not hit. They cowered under the hail of automatic fire.

Racing past the pinned agents, Pierre and the men behind him ran up the steep tortuous path with all the speed they could muster. They had to get to the van!

Behind them, the helicopter had swerved around the beach to the western edge, turned, and swooped low over the water again. As it flew past, men fired from the open door at the men running on the beach. They ducked and lay still under the hail of fire from above. Thinking they'd hit them all, the pilot proceeded to his next assignment.

"Now for the cliff top and that van!" he said to his copilot.

"We've destroyed them!" Laughing triumphantly, he pulled the swirling craft up in a steep climb and poured on the power. The helicopter soared up, up, and over the cliff.

To their complete surprise and shock, they spotted the van racing away in a trail of dust marking.

"They're escaping!" the copilot shouted, pointing to the van as it careened madly along the rough trail.

"Not any more they're not!" the pilot said grimly. "We'll stop them!"

The copilot and his two companions fed fresh clips of ammunition into their automatic rifles as the helicopter caught up to the fleeing van. Racing just over the trees that lined part of the path, the pilot looked for an open place so his men could shoot.

"Just get the driver!" he shouted. "Don't blow up the engine! We want to get those drugs intact!"

"Right," the copilot answered. "Put us alongside the van and we'll pick him off."

The pilot grinned at his companion's confidence in his marksmanship from the air. He knew the man was not boasting. Grimly he maneuvered the helicopter closer to the escaping vehicle, slowing down as he did so to match the speed of his target.

Elated at his escape, thinking he was safely away from the armed men on the beach, Mark was shocked to hear the attacking chopper. Suddenly he saw a burst of automatic gunfire ricochet off the rocky path ahead of him!

He jammed on the brakes, and the helicopter shot past, overreaching him.

Cursing, the pilot pulled the craft around to the left in a wide turn, and prepared to make another attack.

Mark hit the accelerator as soon as the helicopter sped past him. How could he get away from that thing? He raced at top speed for the next group of trees, knowing those marksmen would have a harder time hitting him under the cover of trees if he could get there in time!

And he had no weapon! There was no way he could defend himself from those armed men in the helicopter!

Then he thought of the flares. Grabbing up the pack, he ripped open the cover while his knee jammed against the wheel to keep the racing van on the trail. Pulling out a flare, he searched frantically in the rearview mirror. The helicopter was right on him, just twenty yards behind and about to come alongside.

He waited until the craft was almost parallel to him,

then hit the brakes again, and fired the flare out the open window at the onrushing helicopter.

The flare whizzed by the cockpit of the pursuing craft, shocking the pilot into a sudden pull for altitude and a violent turn to the left. The flare zoomed past as the helicopter turned, climbing into the sky before it burst into a brilliant ball of flame, visible for miles.

"He's shooting flares!" the copilot shouted. "That'll bring the coastal patrols!"

"We've got to get him before he fires another!" the pilot shouted back, as he kept the helicopter in its turn and came back above and behind the racing van. But just ahead was a thick stretch of tall trees through which the rough auto trail disappeared. The van could lose itself in that forest for several minutes if they didn't stop it first!

With intense concentration the pilot brought the helicopter low over the ground, racing to catch the van before it reached the shelter of those tall trees. The men readied their automatic rifles. They *had* to stop that van, recover the drugs inside, and get away before the French police or armed forces learned of the drug war right on their own coast!

Back at the beach, the sudden sound of the attacking helicopter and boat and the waves of automatic rifle fire from the beach had paralyzed David and Penny. They couldn't see any of it from behind the tall rock rising from the water. David's hand was still on the key but he didn't turn it.

"What's going on?" he said, jumping out of the boat, and peering around the rock. Instantly he called to her. "Out of the boat, Penny! Get behind those rocks! A helicopter and a boat are attacking the men on the beach!"

He clambered out, threw the bow line over the stones from which he'd lifted it a moment before, and dashed after her. They scrambled around a pile of stones and stopped to look back at the beach. Kneeling together, his arm around her shoulder, they watched in shocked silence as the gangs blazed away at each other with murderous fire from the automatic rifles. They saw Sergei and Marcel fleeing for cover, exchanging fire with several men on the beach. Others were firing at the helicopter as it swooped low in deadly passes, spewing bullets from the automatic rifles held by the crew.

The helicopter made another pass along the beach. Then it swooped upward and disappeared over the cliff.

Two men kneeling on the beach aimed their automatic rifles and directed a deadly fire against the black boat speeding by. Penny and David watched in shock as flames suddenly leaped up from the engine! Instantly men began to jump from the hurtling craft. Then a violent explosion tore the air! Fire, smoke and pieces of boat shot into the sky and began to rain on the water and on the beach. A circular shock wave moved out across the water's surface from the spot where the black boat had been a moment before.

David knew this was the time to flee. "Penny, we've

got to get away while they're all stunned and while that helicopter's gone! Throw off the line while I start the engine!"

Penny ran to the bow while David jumped again into the driver's seat and scanned the controls. She jumped back on the deck and climbed into the seat next to him.

"Hold on!" he said as he turned the key. The engine came to life. David moved the throttle and eased the boat directly ahead toward the sea.

"As soon as we get around this big rock to the left, they'll see us from the beach, but they won't see us for long because we'll turn right and go around these rock cliffs. Just pray that we'll get that far before they can shoot!"

He moved the throttle to full power, the engine roared to a deafening pitch, and the bow of the boat came quickly out of the water. Huge waves curled upward and outward from the craft as it leaped across the brilliant blue water, gathering speed with each second.

Penny grabbed the side of the boat and held on as it lifted, tilted violently left, then right, and roared out to sea with increasing speed. Craning her neck, she looked back, her anxious eyes searching the beach.

Would anyone shoot them before they were behind the rock cliff?

CHAPTER 17

ESCAPE!

Mark steered the violently lurching van toward the avenue of trees. He *had* to get under their cover before the helicopter made another pass and shot him off the road!

But the chopper was closing fast. Looking in the side view mirror Mark saw the small image grow larger with frightening speed. Soon it would attack.

Suddenly another thought hit him—even if he made it to the trees, he wouldn't know where the helicopter was. It could go ahead, land, and men with guns would ambush him as he came by. And he couldn't drive under the cover of those trees forever. They had to end somewhere.

Glancing in the mirror he saw that the helicopter was on him again! He jammed the brakes, fighting the wheel to keep the rocking vehicle on the road as it slowed drastically. Once more the helicopter went past its target too fast. Again the bursts of automatic weapon fire from the cabin tore up the ground for yards in front of the slowing van.

The enraged pilot cursed violently as he pulled the craft into a tight turn to the left and swept around for another pass. "We'll pull up just when we reach the trees—he'll do the same, since it's the only maneuver he can make on that road; then you guys can shoot him to pieces! One more pass will do it!"

Frustrated again, the three men in the swirling craft checked their guns, jamming full clips of ammunition into them. They'd be ready this time! When that van stopped suddenly again, they'd stop too—and blow the driver off the road! Then they'd land, grab the boxes of drugs out of the van, throw them in the helicopter, and head for home—before the French coastal forces even knew anything had happened at their peaceful beach!

The trees were so close!

Mark had jammed the accelerator to the floor once again, and the vehicle was racing madly for their shelter. Those trees were close—but not close enough. Glancing frantically in the mirror he saw that the helicopter would win the race. He had to do something different.

But what? They'd expect him to slow down since that's all he could do, and that's what he had done before. This time they'd allow for that maneuver. They'd slow down too and shoot him off the road.

But his dad had always told him: "Do what people *don't* expect! Surprise wins more fights than we'll ever know. Do the unexpected!"

He picked up the two remaining flares with his right hand, gripped the ends of the package in his teeth, and tore them off. Now he was ready with the only weapons he had.

Then he had an idea! He slowed the speed of the racing van—not enough to be noticed from the air, but enough to give him an edge when he hit the gas again.

The aircraft was on him, zooming in just fifteen yards to his left, not far from the ground. Two men leaned out of the cabin, guns pointed, ready to destroy him.

Mark hit the brakes, as the men in the helicopter expected him to do. The van skidded and lurched from side to side. Then he stomped the accelerator, and the vehicle bolted forward!

The pilot laughed when the van slowed suddenly. He'd slowed his own craft also. His men laughed as they aimed their guns. This time they had their victim!

But when the van accelerated, the helicopter was caught by surprise and was completely out of position. Cursing, the pilot poured on power in hot pursuit, quickly overtaking the speeding van just at it approached the tall trees.

Mark jammed his knee against the wheel, momentarily holding the van on course. Then he used both hands to fire off the two flares in rapid succession, aiming them at the looming helicopter that was now just a few yards away and above him in the air.

The first flare flashed over the chopper's cabin. The pilot ducked instinctively.

As he did, he dipped the nose of the helicopter downward. The second flare went into the cabin through the open door and between the heads of the riflemen. Hitting an instrument panel just behind the pilot's seat, the flare exploded.

The craft wobbled with the pilot's frantic gyrations to escape the flames in the cabin, and shuddered to a slow stop in the air. Men tumbled out of the burning cabin and fell the few yards to the ground as the craft seemed to stagger toward the trees. As it hit, the rotors were sheared off, the body of the helicopter smashed into a large trunk—and the grove was devastated by the explosion that followed!

The van rocked with the force of the shock wave that burst through the trees just thirty yards behind; then it veered halfway off the road. Gripping the wheel with all his strength, Mark was barely able to keep the vehicle from crashing into a huge tree.

Two men who'd jumped from the burning helicopter lay injured on the ground. Two others had stumbled to their feet after landing, but were knocked down instantly by the violent explosion. Pieces of the helicopter fuselage began to rain down on the trees and on the ground. Flames shot through the trees as gasoline spread and burned. Dark smoke climbed into the sky.

Mark thanked the Lord for His deliverance as he steered the van at top speed down the tree-lined road. He had to get to a village or house and call for help for Penny and David!

Back at the beach the gunfight continued as the white speedboat dashed suddenly from behind the rock and raced for the open sea. Penny craned her neck to look back at the beach. Would the men there shoot at them before they passed around the rocks at the edge of the harbor?

The riflemen firing at Sergei and Marcel had no time to turn and look at the escaping boat. Facing the water, Sergei and Marcel had nearly exhausted their ammunition as they battled the men who had automatic rifles and a seemingly endless supply of bullets. Charles's men still fired at the KGB agents who were working their way back to the entrance to the rocky path that offered escape to the high ground above.

Pierre and the others of Charles's gang had finally reached the top of the cliff by the other path. Gasping for breath from their desperate race up the steep climb, they rushed toward the place where the van had been parked.

The van was gone! Open-mouthed with astonishment, the men gaped at the empty spot.

"Who stole the van?" Pierre shouted.

"None of our men!" the big man answered. "Some of that gang in the helicopter must have taken it. They've got most of our drugs too!"

Stunned at this catastrophe, the defeat of all their efforts, the men huddled helplessly for a moment, not knowing what to do.

"Quick!" the big man yelled, "We've got to get to the motorboat. It's our only escape now. And it still has a lot of the drugs on board."

Turning, he led the angered and confused men

down the steep path cut in the rocks.

"The shooting has stopped!" one of the men said as they skidded to the bottom and headed for the rocky beach.

"Good!" the big man answered. "Now we can grab those boxes on the beach and get away in our boat!"

They ran out on the rocky shore just in time to see the huge curving wakes behind each side of their white boat as it roared away from the beach.

Then the speeding white craft was out of sight, hidden behind the rock cliff to the right, racing to safety across the brilliant blue Mediterranean waters.

"We've got to get away from here," Charles yelled, "and we've got to move fast—before the police arrive! Round up the other men."

Their dazed companions straggled back, having just driven Sergei and Marcel into the steep path down which they'd come so confidently just a few minutes before.

"Who stole our boat?" Charles yelled, pointing to the sea.

"We don't know!" the shocked men answered. "We were shooting at those guys with the pistols and didn't see who was in the boat."

"Who were those guys with pistols?" Charles asked completely puzzled. "I never saw them before. They don't belong to that gang that sabotaged our plane and attacked us just now! Who were they?"

No one answered. No one knew.

"Who were those three American kids with?" the big man asked. "Did they have anything to do with this?"

"We'll never know," Charles said bitterly. "Might as well forget it."

He surveyed the situation. It was terrible. Their boat was gone. Their van was gone. Two men were injured on the beach. They had to get away—and fast. That meant they couldn't carry the remaining boxes of drugs with them.

"Where's that helicopter?" the big man in black asked the group.

No one answered. No one knew.

"Let's get off this beach before it comes back—and before the police get here!" Charles snapped.

"What about the wounded?" Pierre asked.

"Leave 'em," Charles ordered. "We sure can't carry them up that path. Leave 'em."

The men gathered clips of ammunition lying on the beach, and followed Charles toward the path back up the cliff.

Their effort to recover the drugs, so nearly successful, had ended in complete failure. "What a disaster!" Charles said to no one in particular as they began the steep climb. "What a disaster!"

CHAPTER 18

CLOSING IN

Schmidt sat at his desk, staring at the phone in the stifling air of the darkened apartment. The windows were closed as they always were. Stale cigarette smoke caused the place to reek with a dreadful smell. Ashes tumbled onto the battered table from the overflowing ash trays.

"Where is Sergei?" he asked himself frantically. "Why doesn't the man call?" *I can't wait any longer,* he thought finally. *We're all in danger now.*

He picked up the letter from the desk before him, his thick arm bulging through the white shirt as he studied the names on the list before him. He decided to start with the politicians first, then call the university professors, and then the people in television. What an array of propaganda instruments they represented! What a tragedy if they were exposed as the willing tools of the *new* Russia's KGB!

"We can't let that happen!" he said desperately as he reached for the phone. Lifting the instrument, he began to dial.

There was a knock on the door.

He was a shocked—he wasn't expecting anyone! Still holding the phone in his powerful hand, cigarette dangling from his thick lips, he was puzzled.

The knock was repeated. Slowly he put down the receiver and rose. Moving his bulk with surprising grace across the floor, he reached the door. There he hesitated.

The knock was louder. He opened the door. Four policemen stood outside. Schmidt had waited too long to make his calls.

Far to the south of France, on the coast, in fact, Sergei and Marcel reached the parked Mercedes at last. The race up the path had been tortuous, and the two were exhausted. Sweating and gasping for breath, they leaned against the dark blue sedan.

Suddenly they heard the explosion of the helicopter!

"What was that?" Marcel asked, jumping away from the car and drawing his gun.

"I don't know," Sergei replied, "but let's get out of here."

They jumped into the car, Sergei in the driver's seat, and headed away from the beach which had witnessed their failure. Neither of them even mentioned Uri and Jacques, the two men they'd deserted. They drove at high speed and in profound gloom.

"What will he say when we call?" Marcel asked, worry showing in his thick brutal face. He feared Schmidt's terrible wrath.

"I hate to think of it," Sergei replied, but he could guess. This was the third time Sergei had failed—he wouldn't get another chance. His career was finished. And maybe his life.

Oppressed by the dismal future before him, Sergei steered the Mercedes skillfully along the narrow road, slowing slightly for the curves, increasing speed when he could. His mind was racing faster than the engine, however.

Did he dare reveal his plan to Marcel? What would Marcel do when he broached this idea? Marcel might pull a gun and take him to Schmidt! Should he risk mentioning his plan? Sergei was sweating. Finally, he risked all.

"What would you say if we just kept driving to Marseille and took a boat to North Africa?"

Breathlessly he waited for the answer. He was suggesting that they defect! Would Marcel betray him? Maybe shoot him?

Marcel looked sharply at his companion—was Sergei testing his loyalty to the KGB? Was he trying to trap him? But he saw that Sergei was serious. Their situation was desperate. Marcel knew he had to take a chance.

"Let's do it. We've got no future in Paris now—or in Russia."

Relaxing for the first time in a very long while, the two ex-KGB henchmen drove to freedom. They had plenty of expense money to get them to Africa. And Sergei had connections. They began to think they had a future.

Later that afternoon they approached the great

French seaport of Marseille. Traffic was heavy. But the police had been told to look for a dark blue Mercedes, and the two squad cars had done just that.

Pulling up behind the escaping Mercedes, one car flashed its lights until Sergei slowed and drove to the side of the road. That police car parked in front of the Mercedes and backed up to the car's bumper. The other car parked close behind.

Sergei and Marcel were trapped. And they were sick with fear.

Two men with drawn guns emerged from each squad car. The shorter man from the first car turned to his superior, "Allow me, sir." He walked to the window which Sergei had just opened, pulled out his badge with his free hand—the other held the gun—and spoke in flawless Russian to the grim-faced agents: "Welcome to Marseille, comrades! Get out of the car!"

Shocked, the two men inside the Mercedes looked at each other. Who had betrayed them? Slowly they obeyed.

Earlier that afternoon, Jim and Carolyn Daring had walked into the vacation cottage when the phone rang. Jim Daring picked it up.

"Where are the kids?" a voice demanded instantly.

"It's Henri," he told his wife, who was busy putting down the packages she'd bought.

"They're at the beach taking pictures of birds," Daring replied. "Why?"

"Jim," Henri's voice replied, "there's been dirty work again. The kids are in danger! Stay at the house; we're not far away. Stay there in case the kids arrive."

Instantly alarmed, Daring asked, "What kind of danger, Henri?"

His wife stopped putting away her packages and walked quickly to his side.

"The men who stole Penny's camera case want to talk with the kids about it for some reason. We think it's only to ask if you gave the list of names to the police. But we've traced a call from their boss in Paris to a village near you, and I've brought a team of agents with me. We're about to hit the beach."

"What can I do to help?" Daring asked evenly. But his heart was racing; the youngsters were in danger again!

"Stay right where you are—by the phone. If the kids arrive before we do, bundle them in the car and all of you head for the police station in the village. We're closing fast."

"Right," Daring said. Putting down the phone, he turned to explain the situation to his wife. Then they prayed.

Out on the blue Mediterranean Sea, David steered the incredibly fast boat to freedom. The ride was exhilarating! Tall white waves curved gracefully behind and above the stern of the craft as it sped through the water. Penny held tightly to the copilot's seat and admired the way David steered so that they made great speed but didn't smash to pieces against the waves moving toward the shore. But she couldn't relax.

"What do you think's happening to Mark?" she asked anxiously, concern clouding her dark-brown eyes.

"Don't worry!" David assured her, "he's fine. He's hiding in that tower. No one's about to climb that rock wall with all the gunfire going on! He'll be there, safe and sound, when the police arrive. In fact, that guy's had a quiet vacation at the beach while we've been through all this danger!"

That's what David thought! A frantic Mark was in a restaurant in the village some miles from the beach. He'd finally persuaded the owner to let him use the phone to call the police. The owner found the number for him, and Mark was desperately framing his sentences in French.

On the second ring someone answered, and a bored voice asked him what he wanted. Carefully, Mark explained that there'd been a gun battle at a small beach nearby, and that his sister and friend were still there, hiding from drug smugglers until he could get help.

Somewhat skeptical at first, the woman on the phone at last took his message seriously and connected him with a lieutenant. Briefly Mark told of their walk on the beach, the divers, the men with guns, and then the heavy gunfire and explosions. "I got away in their van!" he finished.

Instantly the policeman was replaced by another

voice. "Yes, we know about this. Police from Paris have just flown in and are already moving to the beach. Just bring the van to our station."

"I think it's loaded with drugs," Mark volunteered. "They were taking boxes from a plane that had gone down just offshore."

"Come right away," the policeman insisted.

"Oui, monsieur," Mark replied.

The restaurant owner gladly told him the way to the police station; Mark wasted no time heading there.

Back at the seashore, Charles and his men, hurrying to escape, looked up in fear and yelled. The four F-8Es from the French aircraft carrier *Clemenceau* roared over the beach from the west, creating sonic booms that pounded the rocky shore. The wounded men lying there were shocked by the sound, but helpless to do anything about it. The fighters streaked out to sea as the lead pilot radioed his observations to the police helicopter that directed the aerial part of the joint military and police operation. Then the fighter planes roared back.

Shortly after the fighters' third pass, helicopters arrived at the beach. Two landed on the shore, one at each end; armed men jumped out and began to scout. Two helicopters came to the cliffs above, landed, deployed eight soldiers each, and then took off again to scout the area.

Four police cars jammed to a halt at the top of the cliff. Armed men emerged and quickly fanned out. Some ran for the paths to the beach; others scouted the area at the top for remaining members of the rival drug gangs. With directions from the fighters, a group of police got back in their car and drove to the site of the crashed helicopter. They found there four wounded men and called for a helicopter to retrieve them.

Racing across the blue sea toward the west, Penny and David had seen the jets coming toward them, low over the water, moving with great speed.

"Look, Penny," David cried excitedly, "they're French navy fighters!"

"How can you tell?" she asked as the planes flashed low over the water to their left and rocked them a moment later with the sonic booms.

"What do you mean, 'How can I tell?'" he protested. "Don't you realize I know fighters when I see them? I study planes all the time! They're French navy fighters from an aircraft carrier."

"Look," she said pointing, "they're going right over the beach we left! Oh, David, won't they encourage Mark in that tower!"

"They sure will! I bet the French authorities have found out what's going on! Now those thugs will get what they deserve."

Penny watched, mesmerized, as the planes swooped past the beach, turned gracefully out to sea, then returned to the beach again. And again.

"They're pinning those guys down so they can't get away!" David observed as she described the planes' maneuvers.

That was exactly what they were doing. Charles and his gang had not gotten far from the clifftop when the fighter planes roared over, forcing the men to dive for cover. Before they'd figured out what was going on, the planes came over again. Then the fighters split in pairs, and started back from different directions.

"That's the navy!" Pierre shouted, cowering under a bush. "Who called them?"

"I don't know," Charles replied, as the fighters zoomed over them again, "but it doesn't much matter. We can't move while they're overhead."

That's when they heard the helicopters coming.

"It's all over," Charles said to no one in particular. The men stood up, hands held high, as one of the helicopters landed. Armed men got out and surrounded the defeated gang.

Far to the west, still moving at high speed, David steered the powerful boat toward the docks of a fishing village.

"Oh, David, I know Mark's safe now!" Penny said happily.

"Of course he is!" he replied, laughing at her.

He looked at her again for a long moment. She smiled back, wondering what he was thinking as his dark brown eyes looked into her own.

He was thinking how lovely she looked with her eyes shining and the wind whipping her hair about her face as the speedboat took them to safety. Now that they knew Mark was safe, it was a shame this boat trip had to end! He wondered for a moment how he could string it out; then he realized they had to get to shore and call the police and her parents. He sighed regretfully.

"Mark has had a ringside seat, but he couldn't look out from that tower or the gunmen would have seen him. We'll have to tease him for being so timid while *we* made a getaway and raced for help. Boy, he'll never hear the end of this! In fact, we could make a good story out of it: hand to hand combat with the gang, you pushing one of the men in the water while I threw his buddy out of the boat. Let's plan something spectacular."

She laughed with him and continued looking at his face as he turned the boat toward the approaching dock and slowed its speed.

She couldn't help asking, "Why do guys always make fun of each other and challenge each other? Mom says they all do that, not just you and Mark."

He laughed back as he thought about her question. "Well, we've got to keep each other on our toes, that's why. Can't let a guy relax. He might get lazy or smug, and then he wouldn't be watching out for danger to women and children. And then nice girls like you wouldn't be safe! So we've got to keep each other on guard, all the time!"

He said it in a joking way. Yet she knew that there was real truth in what he said. Her father had told her the same thing many times. "Boys and men have to keep striving to achieve, to improve their skills, and to exert their strength," he'd said. "That's one of the reasons we've raised you differently than we've raised Mark," her father had reminded her. "Girls don't need that kind of stimulus to mature, but boys do. It challenges them to achieve."

Then he told her something he mentioned rather frequently. "Penny, don't waste your time with a boy who's not improving some vital area in his life, or who's not learning. He's not good enough for you."

Poor guys, she thought. *Yet they seem to thrive on it.* Puzzled, not for the first time, and certainly not for the last, at the incredible differences between girls and boys, she shook her head. She was glad the Lord had made her a girl!

CHAPTER 19

ON TO ATHENS

That evening the Daring family, David, and Henri sat in the small dining room of the vacation cottage Henri had loaned them. Carolyn and Penny had cooked a really splendid French meal. As they ate in the leisurely Gallic fashion, Henri had told them the story of the end of the drug gang.

"When we got that list you mailed me, Jim," Henri said, "we knew at once what it meant. A few of those people had worked for the KGB—but not all of them. And we didn't know their connection with each other."

He shook his head. "To think that our beloved country has so many people who are willing to betray her and serve that evil empire to the east! The danger from that empire is not over yet, although the media in our country and yours tell people that it is. The most dangerous part of this century may be ahead of us now!"

Jim Daring agreed. "I think you may be right, Henri."

Like many Frenchmen, Henri moved his head and hands a great deal when he was talking. "We put together a team at once and flew down from Paris. Other police went for the man we knew to be the coordinator, a man named Schmidt. Well, we caught

Schmidt—he was completely surprised! And on his desk was the same list of people that you'd found in Penny's camera case. Our police rounded up a third of those people—we'd planned to get them because of the evidence we already had. And the rest are under surveillance.

"But how did you know to bring all those police to the beach?" Mark asked.

Henri shook his head. "That was a real break! Yesterday, one of our navy's reconnaissance planes spotted an aircraft under the water off this beach. They alerted both the police and the military. That's why our forces were so ready when two boats and a helicopter moved to the beach this afternoon."

He waved his fork in the air with an incredulous expression. "The kids had gotten themselves in the middle of a drug war! Two drug rings based in North Africa were fighting each other for the contents of that sunken plane. Then they found themselves stalked by those four KGB agents. And you three were in the middle of it! And it all happened on the beach where I said you'd have a peaceful time watching birds!"

Henri put down his fork and looked at the three teens. "How do you do it?" he asked, seriously. "How do you get in all these scrapes?"

Before they could answer, he went on. "So we were all ready to coordinate our efforts against that war on the beach. But you three beat us to it and escaped by yourselves!" He shook his head in wonder.

"But how in the world did that list of names get in Penny's camera case?" Carolyn Daring asked, going back to the origin of the trouble. How had her children, and David, come once again into such danger?

"That's the strangest part of all, Carolyn!" Henri beamed, his thin moustache slanting up with his broad smile. "One of the spies we captured in Paris told us. It was placed there the day you left Paris, while you three kids were sitting at an outdoor restaurant. Just before you returned to the hotel, and all of you took the train to Marseille!"

"But who put It there?" Penny asked in astonishment. "I never saw anyone touch it."

"You couldn't, Penny," Henri replied, "because it was behind you. Hanging on the back of your chair while you and the boys talked to Sandra. A woman used that letter to free her son from the KGB. He'd been part of a group sympathetic to the Soviets in the past, and had somehow gotten the information. Then, with the apparent collapse of the Soviet Union, he'd come to his senses and tried to get out of their clutches. But they wouldn't let him go! So he sneaked that list of names to his mother just before they captured him. She knew those people, and made them exchange her son for the list."

"But that still doesn't explain why she put it in Penny's camera case, does it?" Mark asked.

"She hid it there when the man she was meeting came to make a deal with her. She knew they might kidnap her and just take it if she had it on her; so she stuck it temporarily in Penny's camera case and planned to retrieve it when she saw the men deliver her son. But you three left the restaurant before she realized it! She barely saw you get in a taxi!" He laughed at this.

"That made them frantic! The KGB agents rushed after you in another cab, followed you to Marseille, and, as you know, tried to steal it from Penny there. Then they shadowed you in Carcassone and finally followed you here."

"Did the police catch them all?" David asked.

"We think so," Henri replied. "We caught some wounded men on the beach. The soldiers rounded up another gang escaping by foot—David and Penny had stolen their boat! Five others had a hard swim out of the harbor when their boat blew up and we caught them on shore. Just outside Marseille we captured two KGB men escaping in the blue Mercedes we learned about from one of the people we'd captured in Paris. And, we found four others from the helicopter this young man destroyed!"

The Frenchman shook his head in wonder. "You told me, Mark, but I still can't understand how you did it. What a feat!"

"Mark destroyed a helicopter?" David asked incredulously, looking sharply at his friend. "But we thought you were hiding in that tower and couldn't get out until we got help! Penny was frantic worrying about you!"

David and Penny stared at Mark in amazement. So much for their plan to tease him about hiding safely in

a tower while they braved danger and went for help!
"How in the world did you do *that?*" Penny asked,
her eyes wide.

Mark shrugged his shoulders. "Guess I got bored,"
he said.

"Oh, Mark!" Penny said admiringly. "What a
brother you are!" She jumped up and hugged him
tightly. David grinned a rueful grin and gripped Mark's
strong hand.

Henri concluded, "This is an incredible haul of drug
dealers and spies! Two rival gangs were fighting in that
harbor. And four KGB agents were after the kids. And
we got them all!"

Jim Daring brought them back to the subject that
concerned them the most.

"But why did they keep pursuing the kids, once they
got that list of names? What else did they need?"

Henri's face grew sober. "They needed to know if
you had given those names to the police," he said.
"They meant to capture one of you, and find that out."

No one said anything. Penny shivered.

"That settles it!" Carolyn Daring said emphatically,
rising to remove the dinner plates so she could serve
the chocolate pie Penny had made. "That settles it, Jim!
We've got to get these children out of France. The
whole time they've been in danger, and we thought
they'd be safe here!"

"You're right, honey," he said soberly. "I've already
thought of that. I'll take them to Athens with me when

I go to see Alexander Spirodes next week. They'll certainly be safe there!"

"What are you seeing him for, Dad?" Mark asked, excitement obvious in his voice. He couldn't believe it. They were going to Athens, Greece!

Penny and David looked at each other—Athens! Her face broke into a beautiful smile. When David tore his eyes away, he saw Henri grinning at him. David's face got red.

"Alexander Spirodes is a remarkable man, Mark," his father replied. "And he's one of the men investing in our project in Egypt."

The three kids looked at each other. They'd been at that project just two weeks before! And barely escaped!

Jim Daring continued. "Alex has asked me to come see him. He wants to put more money into our Egyptian venture, as well as have us consider a job for his firm in Greece. I'll be there four or five days and can take these three with me while you go back to the little ones in Africa, Carolyn."

"Jim, I'd really thought of their going back with me," she said with concern in her voice. "Do you think this is best?"

"Well, I can't see why not. Paul Froede's going to fly you home to Africa, and bring Rush back to his office in Cairo. The kids and I will be gone less than a week. And nothing could be safer than the home of the Spirodes. You know Sofia Spirodes won't let them get in trouble!"

Later that evening, Mark, Penny, and David took a walk. The three were wild with excitement at the prospect of accompanying Jim Daring to Greece.

"Wow!" Penny said, awestruck. "Imagine going to Athens!"

"That's the cradle of Western Civilization," Mark replied.

"It's incredible history! All the beautiful temples and buildings!" David added. They strolled down the path from the cottage.

"Well, we certainly don't have any enemies there!" Penny said.

"I wonder if we could go sailing while we're there?" David asked. "That's one of their great sports, and those are the seas Ulysses and Themistocles sailed!" He kept glancing at Penny as the three friends walked slowly back to the cottage.

What a pleasant vacation waited for them in Greece.

And that wasn't all!

DARING ADVENTURE #6 PROMO

Awesome Adventures With the Daring Family!

Everywhere Mark and Penny Daring and their friend David go, there's sure to be lots of action, mystery and suspense! They often find themselves in the most unpredictable, hair-raising situations. Join them on each of their faith-building voyages in the Daring Adventure series as they learn to rely on each other and, most importantly, God!

Ambushed in Africa

An attempted kidnapping! A daring rescue! A breathtaking chase through crocodile-infested waters! Can the trio outwit the criminals before the top secret African diamond mine surveys are stolen?

Trapped in Pharaoh's Tomb

The kids are trapped in an ancient Egyptian tomb. How will they escape before the air runs out? Will they be able to outsmart their rival?

Stalked in the Catacombs

Penny, Mark and David explore Paris ...but their adversary is lurking in the shadows. Will they be able to outrun him through the dark catacombs beneath the streets of the city?

Available at your favorite local Christian bookstore.